Panic on the Promenade

Suddenly, between Darm and Babe, a monster appeared on the Promenade. It roared up in front of Darm, black horns shining, red tail whipping from side to side.

People saw the raging purple monster and ran. There was mass panic on the Promenade as the crowd began to run in all directions, tripping over one another in their hurry to escape.

The commotion brought Jake and Nog rushing out of the holoshop.

"Babe," Jake yelled. "Where is he?"

"There!" Nog pointed down the concourse, toward where their furry friend was running for the stairs, dodging between legs of fleeing patrons.

Jake started to run.

The monster vanished.

Then, as Jake looked around, he realized that Babe had disappeared, too.

"If Darm has Babe, then he'll try to sell him to that alien he was with at Quark's," Jake guessed.

"Then let's find the alien and ask him."

"He won't tell us anything," Jake warned.

"He will if we ask him right," Nog said. He used the broad Ferengi grin that meant he had a plan. And that usually meant trouble for someone. . . .

Star Trek: The Next Generation

Starfleet Academy

#1 Worf's First Adventure
#2 Line of Fire
#3 Survival
#4 Capture the Flag
#5 Atlantis Station

Star Trek: Deep Space Nine

#1 The Star Ghost
#2 Stowaways
#3 Prisoners of Peace
#4 The Pet

Available from MINSTREL Books

STAR TREK
DEEP SPACE NINE®

THE PET

MEL GILDEN
and
TED PEDERSEN

Interior illustrations by
Todd Cameron Hamilton

A MINSTREL® BOOK

PUBLISHED BY POCKET BOOKS

New York   London   Toronto   Sydney   Tokyo   Singapore

This book is a work of fiction. Names, characters, places and incidents are either products of the author's imagination or are used fictitiously. Any resemblance to actual events or locales or persons, living or dead, is entirely coincidental.

A MINSTREL PAPERBACK *Original*

A Minstrel Book published by
POCKET BOOKS, a division of Simon & Schuster Inc.
1230 Avenue of the Americas, New York, NY 10020

This book is published by Pocket Books, a division of
Simon & Schuster Inc., under exclusive license from
Paramount Pictures.

ISBN: 0-671-88352-6

First Minstrel Books printing December 1994

10 9 8 7 6 5 4 3 2 1

A MINSTREL BOOK and colophon are registered trademarks
of Simon & Schuster Inc.

Cover art by Alan Gutierrez

Printed in the U.S.A.

For Phillip—keep on Trekin'
                              —Mel

For Phyllis—here's one more pet
to add to the menagerie
                              —Ted

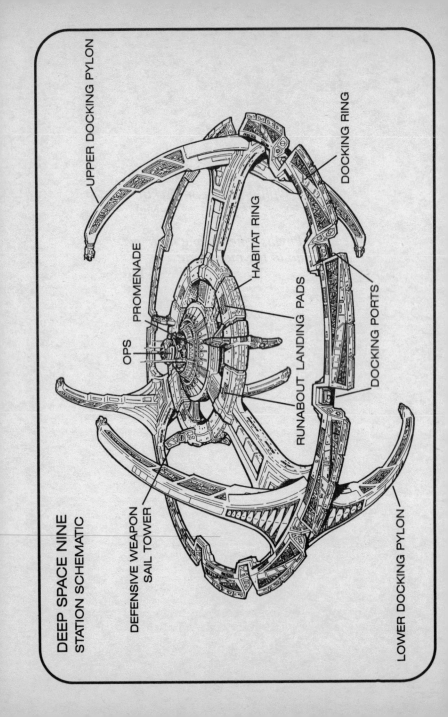

DEEP SPACE NINE
STATION SCHEMATIC

UPPER DOCKING PYLON

DOCKING RING

HABITAT RING

PROMENADE

OPS

RUNABOUT LANDING PADS

DOCKING PORTS

DEFENSIVE WEAPON
SAIL TOWER

LOWER DOCKING PYLON

STAR TREK®: DEEP SPACE NINE™

Cast of Characters

JAKE SISKO—Jake is a young teenager and the only human boy permanently on board Deep Space Nine. Jake's mother died when he was very young. He came to the space station with his father but found very few kids his own age. He doesn't remember life on Earth, but he loves baseball and candy bars, and he hates homework. His father doesn't approve of his friendship with Nog.

NOG—He is a Ferengi boy whose primary goal in life— like all Ferengi—is to make money. His father, Rom, is frequently away on business, which is fine with Nog. His uncle, Quark, keeps an eye on him. Nog thinks humans are odd with their notions of trust and favors and friendship. He doesn't always understand Jake, but since his father forbids him to hang out with the human boy, Nog and Jake are best friends. Nog loves to play tricks on people, but he tries to avoid Odo whenever possible.

COMMANDER BENJAMIN SISKO—Jake's father has been appointed by Starfleet Command to oversee the operations of the space station and act as a liaison between the Federation and Bajor. His wife was killed in a Borg attack, and he is raising Jake by himself. He is a very busy man who always tries to make time for his son.

ODO—The security officer was found by Bajoran scientists years ago, but Odo has no idea where he originally came from. He is a shape-shifter, and thus can assume any shape for a period of time. He normally maintains a vaguely human appearance but every sixteen hours he must revert to his natural liquid state. He has no patience for lawbreakers and less for Ferengi.

MAJOR KIRA NERYS—Kira was a freedom fighter in the Bajoran underground during the Cardassian occupation of Bajor. She now represents Bajoran interests aboard the station and is Sisko's first officer. Her temper is legendary.

LIEUTENANT JADZIA DAX—An old friend of Commander Sisko's, the science officer Dax is actually two joined entities known as the Trill. There is a separate consciousness—a symbiont—in the young female host's body. Sisko knew the symbiont Dax in a previous host, which was a "he."

DR. JULIAN BASHIR—Eager for adventure, Doctor Bashir graduated at the top of his class and requested a deep-space posting. His enthusiasm sometimes gets him into trouble.

MILES O'BRIEN—Formerly the Transporter Chief aboard the *U.S.S. Enterprise,* O'Brien is now Chief of Operations on Deep Space Nine.

KEIKO O'BRIEN—Keiko was a botanist on the *Enterprise,* but she moved to the station with her husband and her young daughter, Molly. Since there is little use for her botany skills on the station, she is the teacher for all of the permanent and traveling students.

QUARK—Nog's uncle and a Ferengi businessman by trade, Quark runs his own combination restaurant/casino/holosuite venue on the Promenade, the central meeting place for much of the activity on the station. Quark has his hand in every deal on board and usually manages to stay just one step ahead of the law—usually in the shape of Odo.

THE PET

CHAPTER I

Play ball!"

The umpire's thunderous voice echoed through Yankee Stadium. The crowd rose as one. *He* was coming.

Young Jake Sisko fidgeted on the pitcher's mound and wiped the sweat from his brow with the back of his hand. Not that he was nervous, but it was the middle of July in New York City and the heat was sweltering.

How did they survive without climate control? Jake wondered. He hadn't thought about it before, but Earth in the twentieth century was a pretty primitive place.

Jake studied the faces of the crowd. They were eagerly waiting for this moment—even the aliens. *Dad is really going to jump all over Quark for programming aliens into his baseball hologame,* Jake thought. Commander Benjamin Sisko loved baseball and wanted it played pure. But Ferengi knew as much about baseball as a Bajoran tree toad did, and cared even less. Setting up this holosuite simulation was strictly a business proposition on

1

Quark's part, and a way to keep on the Federation's good side.

"Jake." Benjamin Sisko approached the mound. His manager's uniform was deliberately wrinkled. Jake liked to play baseball because it was about the only time his dad acted like a real kid instead of like a grown-up. Any other time the commander of Deep Space Nine wore a Starfleet uniform that looked as if it had just come fresh from the replicators, which it usually had.

Benjamin Sisko stepped to the mound and whispered to his son. "Pitch him low and inside—like I taught you. Nothing fast and nothing straight."

His dad had told him that a hundred times. Jake couldn't forget if he wanted to. "Gotcha, Dad."

"Coach," the elder Sisko corrected him.

"Sorry. Coach."

Benjamin Sisko left the mound and returned to the dugout, pausing a moment to frown as he looked into the stands and noticed a pair of Ferengi hawking peanuts and lava worms.

On the mound Jake sized up his opponent. The man swinging the bat at home plate didn't look like much of an athlete. He was, to put it bluntly, overweight. More than that, he was *fat*. But Babe Ruth was also perhaps the greatest slugger in the history of baseball. Or so his father had said. Jake was about to discover the truth of that for himself.

Jake's first pitch was a bit too low and too far inside. "Ball one!"

This wasn't quite as easy as practicing in the Iowa

cornfield simulation where his dad had taught him the fundamentals of baseball. For one thing, this pitcher's mound was a lot farther from home plate.

Jake's next throw was right on target and caught the Babe asleep at the plate. "Strike one!"

Another ball. Then another strike. Finally "Ball three!" It was a full count.

By this time Jake was really sweating, and it wasn't from the heat. This pitch was for all the marbles, or was that a different game?

Jake wound up and threw. The ball arced through the air toward the plate. The Babe started his swing.

"Computer. Freeze program."

The baseball stopped six feet from the plate. So did the Babe and everyone else in the stadium.

Benjamin Sisko ran out of the dugout. "O'Brien!" he shouted.

The door to the holosuite appeared in midair between home plate and first base. Chief Engineer O'Brien stepped through and walked halfway across Yankee Stadium in his Starfleet uniform. No one in the stands noticed because they were frozen solid. This really was "time out," Jake thought.

"Sorry," O'Brien apologized when he reached Sisko. "Things are coming apart in Operations. Four ships just docked, and more are on their way through the wormhole. With docking bay six still down for repairs, we're short one slot."

"Some of them will just have to hang out in orbit," Sisko replied. He turned to Jake. It was his turn to apologize. "Sorry, son. We'll have to replay the game another time."

Jake nodded. "Computer, store program and close."

Instantly Yankee Stadium vanished. Jake watched as his father and O'Brien exited the holosuite, then he followed them.

The two Starfleet men quickly caught a turbolift that would take them directly to Operations, the nerve center that controlled all the technical functions of Deep Space Nine. It was an anniversary of the discovery of the Bajoran wormhole that connected the Federation with Gamma Quadrant, and the celebration was attracting ships from both sides of the wormhole to Deep Space Nine like a magnet.

It was early afternoon, and even if his father had to work, Jake didn't. He hurried to the Promenade to find his Ferengi friend, Nog.

With all these extra ships in dock there was sure to be a lot of excitement on the station.

CHAPTER 2

The first time Jake Sisko saw the creature, it was charging straight toward him. Things like this occasionally happened when Jake played Space Safari with Nog in one of Quark's junior holosuites.

But Jake was not in a holosuite now. Instead he was on Deep Space Nine's main Promenade, an area of exotic shops which was crowded with the passengers and crews from the swarm of starships currently docked and waiting for clearance to pass through the wormhole.

Fortunately, the charging creature was not huge. It was about the size of the Saint Bernard that Jake had played with when his dad took him to the Swiss Alps on their last visit to Earth.

But this didn't look like a Saint Bernard, or any other kind of dog. It reminded Jake of the rhinos that used to roam the African plains, except this creature was covered with a golden fur, from the tip of its stubby horn to the bushy end of its tail.

THE PET

This was all Jake had time to notice as the creature bolted through the crowd on the Promenade, like a rabbit in the woods dodging a pursuing fox, and landed in Jake's lap. Both boy and creature tumbled to the ground.

Jake was scared for a moment, but when he looked into the creature's eyes, he saw that this was no wild beast. This was a being with intelligence. And it was frightened.

Slowly Jake reached out his right hand. He knew what it was like to be alone and afraid. He had felt that way for a long time after his mother had died. He saw that same lonely ache mirrored in this creature's eyes.

The creature responded to Jake's gentle touch and became quiet. For a long moment they sat there face to face, oblivious of the curious crowd that had gathered around them.

"Stop!" An angry cry like thunder shattered the tranquility of the moment. The crowd parted as a big man with black hair and a scar on his left cheek pushed his way through. He was dressed like a spacer, but his manners spoke more of back alleys than of flight decks.

"Stop!" the man yelled again, and the creature cringed as though it had been hit. "Come here!" Despite the harsh command, the creature did not move. It was determined to stay with Jake, as though the young boy could protect him from this angry giant who towered over them.

"The beast is mine," the man said as he glowered at Jake. "Give it to me!"

Jake was too startled to speak. He understood why the creature, or anyone, would be afraid of this man.

The man started to reach past Jake for the creature. "No!"

The familiar voice belonged to Nog. Jake saw his friend running to join them. Nog was pointing at something that the man held in his left hand.

"You can't use a restraining collar," Nog said. "You'll hurt him!" The Ferengi boy tried to grab the collar, but the man pushed Nog aside roughly. The crowd stirred, but no one seemed anxious to take on this enraged spacer.

"It is mine. I do with it what I please."

Jake leaped to his feet, summoned up all his courage, and faced the man. "You can't use a restraining collar on him."

"You'd rather I use it on you?" It was more than a question; it was a threat—and not a subtle one. "Get out of my way, lad!" The man stepped forward. Jake did not move. But what he expected to happen didn't. The man stopped, but not of his own volition. What prevented him from moving was the strong arm of DS9's security chief, Odo. "Shall we discuss this in a civilized manner?"

But the man was not in the mood to discuss anything with anyone. He swung around and attempted to punch his fist into Odo's face—except that Odo's face wasn't there when his fist arrived.

Being a shapeshifter, Odo simply let his face split

apart as though it were liquid. The man's fist went straight through the opening that instantly appeared in the place Odo normally formed his nose.

The man withdrew his fist, muttering a curse against all shapeshifters in general and this one in particular. Then the man lashed out with his right foot.

Odo stepped to one side and used the man's own momentum to send him spinning out of control and to land him flat on his back. In one swift movement Odo put his own foot on the man's throat and applied pressure. The man gasped, turned pale, and went limp. Odo looked over at Jake and smiled reassuringly. "He's all right. I just took the fight out of him."

The constable lifted the man to his feet. He was still gasping. "Though he'll have a sore throat tomorrow morning." Odo looked the man in the eye and demanded an explanation.

"Who—" the man tried to say.

"I'm the law on Deep Space Nine. And you were about to break it."

The man pulled away from Odo's grasp, stumbled, then steadied himself against a bulkhead. Now that the man had, for the moment, lost his will to fight, Odo turned his attention to the gathering crowd. "That will be quite enough. Nothing to gawk at here. Go about your business."

While the crowd slowly dispersed, Nog came over to join Jake, who was gently stroking the distressed creature. The man, regaining his composure, glared at them.

"That thing is mine." He pointed at Jake and Nog. "Those two tried to steal it."

"It—he was frightened," Jake said. "We only wanted to help." Jake indicated the collar lying on the ground. "He was going to use a restraining collar."

Odo picked up the collar and turned to the man. "What you do in space is your business, but this station is Federation territory. And use of a restraining collar requires a permit. Who are you?"

"I'm Darm, third mate of the *Ulysses*. We just came through the wormhole from the Gamma Quadrant. That creature is my property." Darm took a step forward, and the creature quickly sought protection behind Jake and Nog.

"He doesn't appear to like you very much," Odo remarked.

"So what? I know my rights. It belongs to me. I do with it as I please."

Jake and Nog appealed to Odo in unison. "You can't let him take him. He'll hurt him."

Odo considered the quandary. "If Darm does own the creature, then I can't stop him from claiming his property."

Jake shuddered at the thought of this gentle creature in the rough hands of the spacer. Darm smiled with satisfaction and began to step forward, but Odo stopped him.

"On the other hand, I will need to see a legal bill of sale."

"Bill of sale? What're you talkin' about? I picked this thing up wandering around some space rock masquerading as a planet in Gamma Quadrant. I don't have no bill of sale. I don't need no bill of sale. I don't gotta show you no garking bill of sale."

"You say you're off the *Ulysses?*" Odo asked calmly, ignoring the spacer's outburst.

Darm nodded. "Ship's laid up in docking bay eight. Waiting for repairs. Three days I've been stuck on this dump you call a space station."

"Chief O'Brien's a bit overworked at the moment, with all the extra traffic caused by the wormhole celebration. But I'm sure he's doing the best he can." Odo changed the subject. "The *Ulysses,* as I understand it, has been surveying the Gamma Quadrant under a Federation contract."

"So?"

Jake began to smile. Being the son of a Starfleet commander, he understood more about space law than most boys his age. He smiled, sensing what Odo was about to say.

"Under the law, anything brought on board your ship during its mission becomes ship's property." Odo looked over at the creature. "That entity belongs to the *Ulysses.* I'm afraid your captain will have to rule on who owns it."

"You can't do that," Darm protested.

"I can, and I have," Odo said with finality. "Come to Commander Sisko's office with your captain tomorrow morning and we'll settle this."

"But what happens to this little guy until then?" Jake wanted to know as he continued to stroke the golden-haired creature.

Odo scratched his chin and thought. "I don't have an empty holding cell at the moment." Then he smiled to the extent his almost-human features would allow and looked at Jake. "Suppose you two take responsibility for him until then."

Jake and Nog spent the rest of the afternoon with their new friend in their current "secret place," a deserted construction crew module in one of the upper docking pylons.

Deep Space Nine, which was the Starfleet designation for the space station orbiting the planet Bajor, was originally constructed by the Cardassians as a mining operations center. After looting and plundering from the Bajorans until it was no longer profitable to remain, the Cardassians had abandoned the station. But when a permanent wormhole was discovered in the system's Denorios Belt, the station was reactivated by Starfleet as a trading outpost and stopover point for merchants, explorers, scientists, and diplomats going to or coming from the Gamma Quadrant.

Jake's father, Benjamin Sisko, was posted here as commander, and the station was put under Starfleet protection—in case the Cardassians ever decided that it was worth their while to return.

Coming to Deep Space Nine was not really Jake's first choice. He had his heart set on returning to Earth. On the other hand, he wanted to be with his father. And if this is where Starfleet decided they needed Benjamin Sisko, then this was the place Jake would try to call home.

There were not a lot of kids on Deep Space Nine when Jake and his father arrived. There were hardly any people at all. Most everyone who could had already left the space station, either to settle on Bajor or to find a more profitable place to set up shop. Commander Sisko convinced several of the shopkeepers to remain. The most difficult to persuade was Quark, Nog's uncle, who saw no profit in hanging around a decaying planet. But somehow his father had made the Ferengi an offer he couldn't refuse, though he never told Jake what it was.

Whatever it was, Quark reluctantly agreed to stay, and Deep Space Nine reopened for business—though in those first days business was pretty bad.

But then the Bajoran wormhole was discovered, and the shortcut to the Gamma Quadrant opened a whole new universe of opportunity. Gradually more ships passed through the wormhole, and the station population grew. As commerce increased, more families settled on Deep Space Nine until there were enough children to persuade Chief O'Brien's wife, Keiko, to start a school.

Jake, much as he liked to complain, really did enjoy school. His mother had instilled in him her own deep desire to learn. But with his friend Nog it was a different story. That Nog showed up in school at all was a major victory on Keiko's part, with much behind-the-scenes effort by the commander. The Ferengi felt about formal schooling the way Lyorax mud eaters felt about washing —they considered it unnatural.

Nog may have been Ferengi by birth, but he seemed closer to human in attitude. After a couple of false starts, he found that he really liked learning about new things. Their mutual curiosity was the first thing Jake and Nog discovered they had in common.

Desperation originally threw them together, because there was no one else on the station even close to their age. But forming a real bond did not take long. Nog soon became Jake's best friend, and he probably would have been even if they had both been back on Earth.

Now, together with their new alien companion, they climbed the forgotten stairs leading to a small room that was halfway up the inside of the third docking pylon. The room had been stripped of the repair facilities that had once occupied it. A recessed wall table and some storage shelves were the only remaining pieces of furniture.

Jake had discovered this place during one of their "hide-and-seek" games. They immediately adopted it as their clubhouse, though Jake had to explain to Nog what that meant. Ferengi children usually spent their time in more practical pursuits rather than playing out their fantasies in what their parents considered childish, *human* games.

Jake had rigged up some lights and brought in his old hologame projector, while Nog managed to borrow an old replicator from storage. Soon it became their special place, with no one else admitted—until now.

As they stepped inside, Jake had a sudden thought. He looked over at the creature. "We can't keep calling you it—or he. You have to have a name."

"A good Ferengi name," Nog asserted.

"No." Jake looked at the little rhinolike creature, then back at Nog. "No offense, Nog. But it has to be a name that suits him. Names are very important. They tell you a lot about someone."

"So what's his name?"

Jake thought hard for a moment. The name had to be something special. Something appropriate. Suddenly he had it. The perfect name. "Babe."

"Babe?"

Jake nodded. "Babe Ruth was one of baseball's greatest heroes. And, like our friend, a little bit overweight. It suits him. It really does."

Nog wasn't so sure, but having no better idea, he agreed to the name.

"Babe," Jake proclaimed to the alien creature. "You are the first outsider to be invited here."

"Indeed," Nog emphasized, "it is a special privilege. An honor."

Babe wrinkled his fur-covered horn as he surveyed the room. It seemed to Jake that this creature understood what they were saying, although it may have been that he was just naturally curious. They had decided that he was a "he" mainly because otherwise they would have had to break their "no girls allowed" rule.

Soon Babe found a suitable corner on the highest shelf and curled up to take a nap. Jake theorized that Babe may have come from a mountainous world where safety was found in the higher regions. The creature was certainly adept at climbing. Nog suggested that maybe there were a lot of trees on Babe's planet.

Jake and Nog observed the sleeping Babe with growing affection. No matter what they had to do, they agreed that they would not let this gentle creature fall into the hands of someone like Darm. What that might require of them, they had no way of knowing, but Jake and Nog formally sealed their commitment with a sacred oath that they remembered from a hologame, Pirates of the Pleiades.

The rest of the afternoon was occupied by more pleasant pursuits as they played Maze Masters with the hologame projector. Nog, who considered himself a maze master of the first rank, was surprised at how fast Babe figured out the possibilities and emerged from the maze first seven times out of twelve.

Jake, who silently hated coming in second in the maze whenever he played Nog, was beaming at the second-place showing of his Ferengi friend.

Then, Babe apparently noticed the obvious discomfort that Nog was suffering, and Jake thought he saw the creature deliberately lose his way, enabling Nog to win the last three contests. Jake accepted it as a further sign that Babe was more intelligent than the average pet, but Nog insisted that it was simply his superior Ferengi talent rising to the challenge.

When they all tired of the game, they left their clubhouse and visited the observation deck above the

Promenade. This was one of Jake's favorite places. The large windows looked out on the Bajoran solar system and the cosmos beyond. If one made a complete circuit of the upper tier, the overwhelming impression was that Deep Space Nine was indeed an island floating in a vast sea of space. It was a good place not only to see the stars outside, but to watch the throngs of people that crowded the Promenade below.

The wormhole anniversary celebration had attracted as many different groups of humans and aliens as Jake had ever seen assembled in one place. Many of them strolled with their own pets, which ranged from a whistling tyra-bird perched on the shoulder of a portly Sardakan merchant, to a spider-wasp that fluttered around its owner's head, to a pair of six-limbed rim runners that constantly tangled their leashes around the legs of their Bajoran mistress. But none of those other pets, Jake and Nog agreed, could hold a Tjrak candle to Babe.

Since the room that Quark provided for Nog to share with his father, Rom, was, even by Ferengi standards, small, Jake and Nog decided that Babe should stay overnight in the Sisko quarters.

Later that evening, over dinner, Jake mentioned Babe's quick learning abilities to his father.

"I'm not sure that means Babe is intelligent in the sense you mean it," Benjamin Sisko responded. "Morovian rats can learn to navigate a complex maze faster than their owners, but they aren't intelligent in human terms."

"Babe is smarter than any rat," Jake contended.

"I'm sure he is, Jake. In his own way. All of us have our own special talents. Like the skills of a great athlete."

"But didn't you tell me that in baseball the best pitcher is not the one with the *fastest* ball, but the one with the *smartest* ball?"

Benjamin Sisko smiled. "Yes. I did."

The commander glanced over at Babe, who was curled up in his favorite chair. "I have to admit that your friend Babe is certainly smart enough to pick out the best seat in the house."

19

"Dad, why do you think that spacer Darm wanted Babe?" Jake asked, changing the subject. "He doesn't seem like someone who appreciates pets."

"Babe is a rare creature from the Gamma Quadrant. I suspect that Darm planned to sell him."

"Sell him?" Jake was horrified by the thought of Babe being bought and sold like so many self-sealing stenbolts. Jake excused himself and went over to sit next to Babe. He liked that his father called Babe a "friend" rather than a "creature," or even worse—as Darm had said on the Promenade, a "thing." It just wouldn't be right for Babe to belong to someone like that.

Jake watched as his father cleared the table and carried the used dishes to the convertor for recycling. He was certain that the commander of Deep Space Nine would be able to claim Starfleet jurisdiction and keep Darm from getting Babe.

Jake petted the soft golden fur of the alien creature, who responded with a low hum that was not unlike the purr of an Earth cat. Jake became more determined than ever to keep Babe.

CHAPTER 3

Ready?" Nog asked.

"Whenever you are," Jake replied.

Nog nodded, then pitched the small white sphere of the baseball. It left the pitcher's mound and arced through the azure blue Iowa sky toward home plate.

Crack!

Jake swung and the bat made hard contact with the ball. The ball spun out over the grassy meadow toward the distant cornfields.

"Another long one!" Jake smiled as he watched the ball he had just hit whiz past Nog's oversize ears. By the time the Ferengi reacted and made a halfhearted attempt to snare the ball, it was well beyond the reach of his glove. It was a home run for sure. Or would have been.

Suddenly a furry comet leaped high off the ground and snatched the runaway ball out of the air. Babe had done it again.

"I think he likes this game," Nog said as the little rhino-nosed creature proudly deposited his catch at the Ferengi's feet.

Jake smiled at this furry little being who was rapidly becoming an important part of their lives. Babe was certainly an appropriate name. He wondered whether they played baseball on the planet he came from. Jake knew that the meeting in the commander's office was going to turn out well. But just in case it didn't, both he and Nog had wanted to share whatever was left of this special time with Babe.

On the mound Nog was winding up for another pitch. Jake approached the plate, then hesitated. The sun was directly overhead, which meant it was time to end this game.

"Computer, terminate program," Jake said.

The Iowa countryside vanished. Jake and Nog left the holosuite, followed by Babe.

They bypassed the Promenade, which Jake noted was already crowded with the passengers and crews of the small armada of starships arriving to celebrate the anniversary of the wormhole, not to mention a continuing shuttle of Bajorans who took the opportunity of a planet-wide holiday to visit the station.

For most it was their first visit here, but Jake noticed that more than a few were former slaves of the Cardassian masters who once ran Deep Space Nine. Now they came to walk the steel corridors as free men and women.

Nog proudly pointed out that his uncle, Quark, had set up a souvenir stand near the main exit from the docking bays peddling genuine Cardassian artifacts and treasures from the Gamma Quadrant. "Ferengi Rule of Acquisition Number Nine: 'Instinct plus opportunity equals profit.'"

But Jake was reminded of another Ferengi rule: "A bargain usually isn't." The authentic Cardassian artifacts were replicated, and the Gamma Quadrant treasures came from a Kajorak space trader who had drunk too much at Quark's and bet too heavily at the *dabo* wheel.

In spite of the fact that Jake had calculated the time it would take to get from the holosuites to Operations, the meeting had already begun by the time they arrived.

Odo was waiting impatiently for them outside the door to Commander Sisko's office. As he ushered Jake, Nog, and Babe into the office, he quickly explained that the commander and Captain Pavlov of the *Ulysses* had been fully apprised of the situation.

Commander Sisko did not appear to notice their late arrival as he was occupied in conversation with a huge man with a red beard. The spacer, Darm, did notice them and glared silently from across the room. Jake, Nog, and Babe slid quietly into a corner and waited to be called upon.

When there was a lull in the conversation, Benjamin Sisko turned to his son. "Glad you could make it," he said with a soft reprimand.

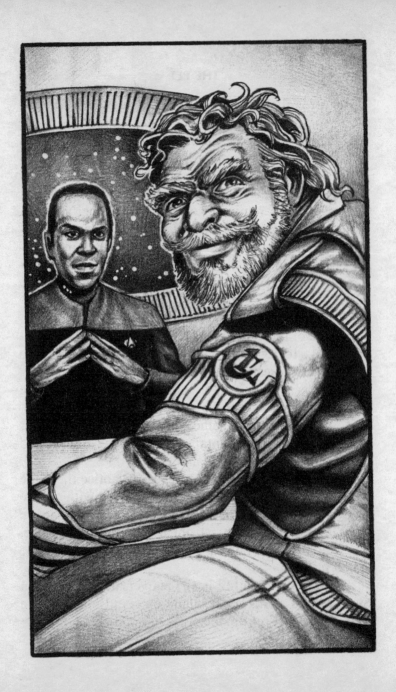

"Sorry, Dad," Jake started to explain, "but the Promenade was really crowded."

Sisko was about to reply, when Captain Pavlov interrupted. "Forgive their tardiness, Commander. They are still boys and enjoy the luxury of their youth." He turned to Jake and Nog and introduced himself, "I am Alexander Pavlov, Captain of the *Ulysses.*"

For the first time Jake took a good look at Alexander Pavlov. He was a great Russian bear of a man who reminded Jake of a picture of a Cossack chieftain from an old history book. He not only occupied the commander's office on the Deep Space Nine Operations bridge, but he dominated it. His long curls and shaggy beard were as flaming red as his temper, which now flared as he returned to the reason he had been called here.

Fortunately his anger was not directed at Jake or Nog, or even at Babe, who lay curled up between them. Nor was he upset that Commander Sisko had summoned him here. No, his anger was clearly aimed at his third officer.

Unlike the day before, Jake noticed that Darm stood silently and accepted his captain's verbal onslaught. It was not a pleasant sight for anyone involved, and Jake almost felt a twinge of compassion for the spacer.

When he had finished reprimanding Darm, which was meant to demonstrate his regret over the matter, Pavlov turned his attention to the commander. "I apologize for the actions of my officer. Darm brought the creature aboard the *Ulysses* without my permission or knowledge."

"I didn't think it was important—" Darm started to speak, then stopped short when the captain glared at him.

"Darm is skilled at his duties," Pavlov continued, "but he has a trait common to free-spacers. He sometimes bends the rules to suit his own ends."

"He must have Ferengi blood in his background." No sooner had Sisko made the remark than Jake saw his father glance over at Nog as if to say that present company was excluded.

Nog only smiled. Jake knew he considered the commander's statement not a slight, but a compliment.

"Returning to the subject at hand," Sisko quickly continued. "We have a situation here that must be resolved."

"Yes," Pavlov agreed. He thought for a moment. "I have spent most of my life on the rim worlds, where we do tend to make our own rules. But this expedition to the Gamma Quadrant was under Federation charter."

He looked down at Babe. "I would return the creature to his homeworld, but that is not possible." He looked over at Darm. "We stopped at many worlds, and my third officer is uncertain as to which one the creature came from." Pavlov stroked his beard. "There is no place for the creature on the *Ulysses.*" He glared at Darm. "And I suspect that my third officer lacks the temperament to keep or care for a pet."

Captain Pavlov smiled at Jake and Nog. "Therefore,

my decision is to transfer custody of the creature to the two lads." He looked at Sisko. "If that meets with your approval, Commander."

"It does. On one condition." Sisko looked at Jake and Nog. "Babe is your responsibility. You must both promise me that you will care for him—and train him so that he does not create a problem on the station."

Jake saw his father's serious expression. Whatever Benjamin Sisko said when he wore that expression, he meant.

"We promise, Dad."

After the meeting Jake and Nog had just enough time to get to school if they didn't drop Babe off at the Sisko quarters. So the furry alien creature spent his first day as an official Deep Space Nine resident accompanying his new masters to class.

Babe was, of course, an immediate hit—even with Keiko O'Brien, who found Babe's presence beneficial in stimulating her young charges into thinking about responsibility. There were very few permanent pets on Deep Space Nine because it was still more of a way station than a family settlement.

"But didn't the early pioneers on Earth take dogs along when they crossed the frontier?" Jake asked.

"Yes, they did. But those dogs were not pets. They were working animals, like the cowboys' horses."

"What's the difference?" asked the daughter of one of the Bajoran shopkeepers.

"Dumb animals," Keiko began, then paused as she smiled at Babe. "I should say 'non-sentient' creatures.

No disrespect to you, Babe. We humans tend to refer to creatures we dominate as 'dumb,' even when many of them are lot smarter than their owners."

Jake hoped she wasn't talking about him and Nog.

"Our animals fall into two categories. The first is the working animal, like the dogs originally bred from wolves that helped early people on Earth hunt or protect their herds. The second, a category which appeared more recently in our history, contains animals that are kept by people as companions. These are pets."

"Babe is our pet," Nog proclaimed proudly.

"Then," replied Keiko, "you have accepted the responsibility to care for him. You and Jake have become his parents."

Jake and Nog traded glances. They understood the seriousness of their responsibility.

"In the beginning it is a lot of fun to have a pet," Keiko continued. "But there will be times when Babe creates problems and you might wish he wasn't around. And there will be a time when he gets old and sick. But he remains your responsibility, and you cannot discard him like a toy that is broken."

"We'd never do that to Babe," Jake assured her.

Keiko smiled. "No, Jake. I know you wouldn't."

When school was out for the day, Jake and Nog hurried to the Promenade with Babe tagging along at their heels. It was still crowded as they made their way toward Quark's.

The shopkeepers and pedestrians they passed were

properly impressed by the golden-horned creature who tagged along behind them, which put Jake and Nog in the mood to celebrate.

Which they did. They sat in a corner of Quark's that was reserved for family groups. It was a rather small corner, with only two tables, since Quark preferred a different clientele. Families gave the place some air of respectability, but respectable folks also tended to keep most of their money in their pockets.

Quark preferred the rough-and-ready types who spent their wages freely, liked their drinks strong, and weren't adverse to trying their luck at the *dabo* wheel. Fortunately for Quark, very few of them had any luck.

"So, nephew, and young Sisko," Quark greeted the boys as they sat down. "What will it be? Something special for a special day?"

There was no hesitation as they replied in unison. "Two Ventaxan Volcano Sundaes." It was a special day, Jake thought. But it was special because of Babe, not the wormhole anniversary.

Quark looked down at Babe. "And for your furry friend?"

Jake hadn't thought about ordering for Babe. He didn't even know what he ate. Except for drinking some water, Babe hadn't eaten anything the day before. Nor did he seem hungry now.

"Nothing," Jake told Quark and shrugged.

When Quark left, Jake leaned over to Nog. "We better not give Babe anything until we have Dr. Bashir check him out. We don't want to make him sick."

"Good idea," Nog agreed.

While waiting for their sundaes, Jake turned his attention to what had become one of his favorite activities on Deep Space Nine—people watching.

The unusual and often outright bizarre travelers that passed through the station stirred Jake's imagination. He liked to speculate on the kind of planets these strange people might have come from, and to imagine the exciting worlds where they might be going.

That two-headed Benzian miner slurping a double dish of some kind of blue soup was a good example. Jake wondered what it would be like to have two heads. Did the two heads ever argue? It would be pretty hard to stomp out of the room and leave your other head behind.

Or the lizard-skinned Alborian salesman who was tallying up his day's orders on a tri-dimensional holoscreen. Jake wanted to pretend the salesman was a weapons dealer operating on the edge of Federation law, though the hologram samples shown on his display looked more like household cleaning gadgets.

But when his gaze fell upon a dark corner of the room, secluded from the rest of Quark's by some thick brown Bajoran flora, Jake saw Darm watching them. The intensity of the spacer's cold glare frightened Jake.

Seated across the table from Darm was a nasty-looking turtle-necked alien who was using his long black tongue to snap up live insects from a slimy heap that looked more like it came from the garbage disposal than from the food replicator.

Jake quickly averted his eyes. "It's Darm," he whispered to Nog.

"Relax," Nog replied. "He's not going to bother us."

But even as Nog was assuring Jake, Darm was crossing the room. Much too soon he stood at their table towering over them like some evil specter.

Babe, who had been quietly resting beneath the table, emerged with what could only have been a growl. Darm took a quick step back but retreated no farther.

"We got off to a bad start. Let's be friends." Darm tried to be nice, but he obviously hadn't had much practice in the art of polite conversation. His offer of friendship was about as sincere as a Horax inviting you to dinner, and forgetting to mention that *you* were going to be the main course.

"Let's not," Nog said.

Darm looked at the small Ferengi. Slowly he turned a grimace into a poor example of a smile. "Okay. Forget friendship. Ferengi are dealers. So let's make a deal."

"What kind of a deal?" Nog asked.

Jake saw Nog's eyes take on that special Ferengi glaze, and knew that in spite of Nog's dislike for this spacer, he was too much a Ferengi to ignore any opportunity to make a profit.

"I'll buy the creature back from you," Darm quickly said, seizing the opportunity.

"He's not for sale," Jake declared.

Darm ignored Jake and aimed his argument at Nog. "I'll give you a handsome profit."

31

"Why would you want Babe?" Nog inquired.

Darm leaned close to the Ferengi's oversize ear. "I shouldn't be telling you this, but you kids got me in kind of a bind." Darm glanced over his shoulder at the insect-eating alien in the corner. "My friend with the strange appetite collects things. Living things. Kind of like a zoo."

Darm pointed to Babe, who was hiding under the table again. "That little creature is a new life form from the Gamma Quadrant, and my friend will pay a lot to add him to his collection."

Dad was right, Jake thought. Darm didn't care about Babe. He only wanted the creature so he could sell him.

Nog actually seemed to be considering Darm's offer, which disturbed Jake. But then Nog's human attributes overcame his inherent Ferengi greed. "No sale. At any price."

"I can make a good deal with my slithery friend over there." Darm threw a look back at where his alien companion was busily snapping up flies. "And I don't want you two ruining it. Sell me the creature or you'll be sorry—very sorry!"

Jake wasn't sure what Darm intended to do next, and he was glad not to have the opportunity to find out, for at that moment Quark arrived with two huge Ventaxan Volcano Sundaes.

Intentionally or not, Quark deposited the two fiery desserts on the table so that the smoke curled up into Darm's face. The spacer coughed, threw a threatening "I'll be back" glare, and stomped off.

"Enjoy," Quark said as he returned to the bar.

Jake and Nog could hardy wait for the burning volcanoes of the Ventaxan dessert to cool. But Babe didn't seem to mind the heat, because he tried to grab a bite of Jake's sundae.

"No," Jake told him. "This isn't healthy for you."

Babe made a low noise that seemed to say "I know what's good for me." Jake might have relented, but Nog reminded him that they needed to check with Dr. Bashir before feeding Babe anything.

"Sorry, Babe," Jake told the creature. "It's for your own good." Jake silently grimaced as he said the words that his father had often used on him, and which he had sworn never to use on someone else.

Apparently satisfied with the reprimand, Babe sat down. Jake and Nog turned their full attention to the sundaes, which were now ready to eat.

So engrossed were the boys in devouring their desserts that they didn't notice what has happening around them until they heard Quark's frantic scream.

"Fire!"

Jake looked up to see that an enormous replica of the Ventaxan Volcano had materialized out of nowhere. It was ten feet high and raging out of control in the middle of the floor, right in front of Babe. Smoke, ash, and a huge column of flame spiraled toward the ceiling.

"Fire!" someone yelled again, but it was certainly unnecessary as the center of Quark's Place seemed to have exploded into flames. Patrons were leaving rapidly, though most had the good sense to take their drinks with

them. The smoke was turning Quark's into a disaster zone.

"The sprinklers! They're supposed to be automatic!" Quark yelled. "I'll have O'Brien's hide for this!"

Nog got up and ran to the manual controls on the wall. "I'll turn them on, Uncle Quark!"

Jake grabbed Babe and pulled him away from the volcano, which was spurting red-hot chocolate lava rocks in all directions. "Babe! Get away!"

At that moment the sprinklers came on. Quark's was drenched in a deluge of fire-quenching liquid.

Nog joined Jake and Babe. "I think we'd better leave," he suggested.

Jake wasn't quite sure how they could be held responsible for this, but the look that Quark was giving them indicated that staying around wasn't a good idea.

As they made their retreat, Jake looked back through the downpour and saw that the volcano was not only out—*it had vanished.*

CHAPTER 4

The day that had begun in the commander's office on such a high note ended there on a much lower one.

Jake, Nog, and Babe sat against the wall awaiting their fate. Jake knew they would not be shot, hung up by their feet, or fed to Cardassian leeches, but that did not prevent him from worrying about how much of the incident at Quark's they would be blamed for. Jake was careful to avert his eyes whenever the commander glanced in his direction while Odo made his report.

"Thank you, Constable," Sisko said when the security chief had finished.

"This is Quark's estimate of damages." Odo handed the document to Sisko, who quickly scanned the list.

"For an estimate, this is certainly detailed." Sisko set the document on the desk, then picked it up again for a second look. "There's no item for fire damage."

"There was none," Odo replied.

"I don't understand. The sprinklers were turned on because there was a fire."

"There *appeared* to be a fire, Commander. The evidence supports the fact that any fire was just that—an appearance."

"I'm not sure what you're telling me, Constable. Was there a fire or wasn't there?"

"To rephrase one of your quaint Earth sayings, where there's smoke, there is not always fire. Nothing in Quark's was burned."

"You're telling me it was a mass hallucination?"

"Given that it was late afternoon and the customers who frequent Quark's are not the most reliable, I suspect that the sight of the flaming dessert ordered by Jake and Nog prompted one of them to believe the establishment was on fire."

"I see. And everyone else panicked before they realized there was nothing to panic about. Thank you, Odo. That will be all." Commander Sisko now turned his attention to Jake and Nog.

"Young man." Jake cringed whenever his father used *that* term. "How do you explain this?"

"We didn't do anything wrong, Commander," Nog insisted.

"I'm not blaming you." The commander replied to Nog, but his gaze remained fixed on his son. The word *yet* was not spoken, but Jake could feel its presence all the same.

"We don't know what happened, Dad. That's the honest truth. All of a sudden there was fire and smoke everywhere. I pulled Babe away from the flames, and Nog turned on the sprinklers."

Sisko stood up and scratched his head. "This whole thing is a puzzle. Everyone says there was a fire, but nothing was burned."

"However, the damage from the fire-quenching spray *is* real," Odo added.

"True. But I can hardly discipline young Nog for trying to prevent what he believed was a disaster."

"What do I tell Quark?"

"That Starfleet will reimburse him for his damages." Sisko picked up the document and handed it to Odo. "His *actual* damages."

"I'll make that quite clear." Odo turned and left the office.

When the door closed, Sisko looked at his son. "I'm not sure exactly what happened at Quark's. But you three seem to be off the hook—for the moment."

"Then we can go?" Jake asked.

"Yes. But try to keep yourselves—and your pet—out of trouble. At least for the rest of the day."

Jake and Nog headed back to the Promenade with Babe tagging along beside them. Jake wasn't quite sure what, if anything, they had actually done. But when adults were involved, a kid didn't always have to do anything to get blamed. Even his dad sometimes responded as though kids were as naturally devious as Ferengi. Which was why the commander had never totally approved of Nog as Jake's best friend.

They took a turbolift that deposited them on the observation deck.

Jake paused in front of the window that faced out onto the location where he knew the wormhole lay, and wondered when he would get a chance to travel through the interstellar tunnel which connected this section of space with the Gamma Quadrant, more than seventy thousand light years away.

Jake used *when* rather than *if,* knowing that sometime he would be going out to the stars, perhaps even to Babe's home planet, wherever it was.

"Somehow," Jake told Nog, "we have to get Babe home again."

"You want to hand over our pet to some stranger after Captain Pavlov gave him to us?" Nog asked.

Jake reached his hand down and gently rubbed the soft fur of Babe's horn. *He must be lonely,* Jake thought. Much as he would hate to part with this new companion, Jake would not hesitate to give him up if there was a way that Babe could go home again. "We have to think of what's best for Babe. He may be lonely for his real owner."

Babe rubbed against his leg as though he understood what Jake was thinking and appreciated the boy's concern. Then, like a puppy with a new world to explore, Babe bounced off and ran ahead of them toward the stairs that led down to the crowded main concourse.

It was evening and Quark had stopped selling souvenirs. He now featured a pair of beautiful Bajoran girls in native costumes beckoning passersby to enter Quark's for a friendly spin at the *dabo* wheel. Now the bright family circus atmosphere of the day had turned to the more garish appeal of a rimworld sidestreet.

Jake noticed that Babe, rather than jogging along at their heels, had become confident enough to wander off on short exploratory jaunts. He never strayed too far, however, as though realizing that his archnemesis, Darm, was still in the neighborhood.

"Jake! Look over there!" Nog stopped short. Jake, who had been watching Babe, almost collided with him.

They were standing in front of three rotating holographic spheres that announced—or rather, *shouted*—their message to potential customers:

HERE NOW!
"MONSTERS OF THE LOST PLANET"
THE ADVENTURE IS ALL IN YOUR MIND!

The spheres, pulsating with all the colors of the rainbow, beckoned the curious to enter the hologame shop. Jake and Nog watched in awe as the advertising message exploded into a preview of the game itself. Daring spacemen fought purple monsters, who sported multiple black horns and scarlet tails that were sharp as spears. The spacemen, who looked surprisingly like Jake and Nog, battled in the craters of a brown desert planet that had three moons in the background.

"That's us!" Nog exclaimed, pointing to the spacemen in the hologram.

Jake nodded knowingly. "The sensor scans whoever is closest and programs their image into the display." In spite of himself, Jake was impressed.

"It's the new game we've been hearing about," Nog said as the preview blinked off.

Jarad the Bajoran shopkeeper stepped up beside them. Most of his products were intended for the same audience that frequented Quark's holosuites and were not really suitable for family audiences. But he did carry a small line of kids' entertainments as a courtesy for the growing number of children on Deep Space Nine and for space travelers who purchased them as homecoming gifts.

"You boys want a demonstration?" Jake and Nog were his best customers for these games. They were granted special privileges because of that, and because they were a good indicator of how well the games would sell.

"We sure would," Jake replied. Nog was already inside the shop.

In their rush to preview the new game, they momentarily forgot about Babe.

Left on his own, Babe began to investigate the Promenade.

At first the sweet smell of Algorian spices lured him. Then he lingered for a while in front of a vendor hawking Orion chanting crystals. The entire Promenade was a carnival of strange scents and colors, each beckoning the creature a little farther from the hologame shop.

Finally Babe's wandering took him to the less crowded far end of the Promenade—where he suddenly stopped short. His horn quivered as he sensed danger. Quickly Babe turned and started back the way he had come.

But the hulking form of Darm stood directly in his path. He faced the little creature like some deadly predator confronting a defenseless victim that has strayed too far from the safety of the herd. Babe backed away.

"Going somewhere, my furry friend?"

Babe may not have comprehended the words, but their intent was crystal clear.

Suddenly, as though driven by panic, the little rhinolike creature dashed toward a side corridor. But the corridor came to an abrupt end at a bulkhead. Babe was trapped.

Darm stood at the entrance to the corridor and slid the restraining collar out from under his tunic. "This is going to hurt you more than it does me," he said with a smirk as he stepped forward.

Like a trapped beast left with no other choice, Babe desperately rushed toward his attacker.

Darm swung the collar like a lasso, but he mistimed the speed of his target. Babe dashed between his legs, spinning Darm off balance and sending him sprawling onto the floor.

"You'll pay for that," Darm cursed. He scrambled to his feet, his face twisted by a raging anger.

Babe found his way blocked by the crowd and darted

toward a shop, but the door was closed. Babe pawed frantically at the door.

"That's as far as you go," Darm said as he approached Babe. "There's nowhere to run."

Babe did not try to run, but instead turned to face his adversary.

Darm seemed to take this as a signal of surrender. He moved forward with confidence.

Suddenly, between Darm and Babe, a monster appeared on the Promenade. It roared up in front of Darm, black horns shining, red tail whipping from side to side.

The spacer screamed, and he wasn't the only one. The single scream multiplied. People saw the raging purple monster and ran.

There was mass panic on the Promenade, pure and simple, as the crowd began to run in all directions, tripping over one another in their hurry to escape.

The commotion brought Jake and Nog rushing out of the holoshop.

"Babe!" Jake yelled. "Where is he?"

"There!" Nog pointed down the concourse, past where the purple monster raged at the crowd, to where their furry friend was running for the stairs, dodging between the legs of fleeing patrons.

Jake started to run, but a security guard stepped in front of him. "No. Let me handle this, son."

The security guard pushed Jake aside. He commanded

people to get out of his way, then stepped into the middle of the concourse and pointed his phaser. He fired a single blast at the monster.

And the monster vanished.

Then, as Jake frantically looked around, he realized that Babe had disappeared, too.

CHAPTER 5

A search of the Promenade turned up nothing. Babe was gone.

Jake and Nog were worried. Their pet was frightened and had probably found a hole to hide in. He could be almost anywhere on the station.

Jake's aunt on Earth had a cat. When Kitty got scared, she could crawl into the smallest and darkest of corners. If Babe had that ability, they might never find him.

"He'll come out when he gets hungry." Nog was certain that food could tempt anyone into anything, but Jake had his doubts. In the almost two days he had known Babe, Jake could not remember seeing the creature actually eat anything.

"Maybe Babe doesn't eat," Jake guessed aloud.

"Of course he eats," Nog insisted. "Everyone has to eat something."

"I hope you're right."

"Trust me. The Ferengi know food."

Jake suddenly had an unwelcome thought. "You don't suppose Darm got him, do you?"

"Let's have Odo check."

Unfortunately Odo was otherwise occupied when the boys found him outside Quark's. He was trying to sort out the affair of the vanishing monster, and from the tone of his conversation it was clear that Odo believed the Ferengi merchant was somehow involved.

"How can you possibly suspect me?" Quark demanded, doing his best to seem outraged by the mere suggestion of impropriety.

"Because," Odo replied, "you have been doing everything in your power to make a profit during the wormhole celebration."

"Of course I am. No Ferengi would ever let such an opportunity pass without participating in some meaningful way."

"So you admit it?" Odo asked.

"I admit nothing," Quark answered. He pointed at the sparse crowds on the Promenade. "Why would I do something that would drive my potential customers away?"

Odo reluctantly had to agree that the monster's appearance had not increased Quark's business.

Seeing that Deep Space Nine's security chief was finished with Quark, Jake and Nog seized the opportunity to ask for Odo's help in finding their missing pet.

Jake explained that Darm had been on the Promenade

when Babe disappeared. Nog added that they were certain the spacer was involved.

While Odo sympathized with the boys' concern and even agreed that Darm might be mixed up in Babe's disappearance, he had to finish this current investigation before starting a new one.

"It's very likely that Babe is just hiding," Odo tried to reassure them as he left to talk with other pedestrians who had seen the monster.

Except, if Darm really did kidnap Babe, Jake was afraid that they might already be too late. With all the adults busy with what they considered to be a more important problem, Jake and Nog were on their own.

"We need to play detective," Jake said.

"Like in *Sherlock Holmes and the Cardassian Corpse?*" Nog asked. "That holovid we watched last week?"

Jake nodded. Both boys sat down on a bench and tried to think of what Sherlock Holmes and his companion, Watson, would have done.

"If he does have Babe, then he'll try to sell him to that alien fellow he was with at Quark's," Jake guessed.

"Then let's find the alien and ask him."

"He won't tell us anything," Jake warned.

"He will if we ask him right," Nog said. He used the broad Ferengi grin that meant he had a plan. And that usually meant trouble for someone.

The alien, Nog had discovered from his uncle, Quark, was a Xaranian merchant who went by the name of

Forsh. They found him half submerged in a mud bath in the Bajoran health spa across from Quark's. Actually, he wasn't alone. A dozen swamp slugs wriggled in the blue-green muck along with him.

"They cleanse the body," Forsh told them. "You should try it sometime."

Jake was doing his best to look somewhere else. While he knew taking a slime bath was not a totally uncommon alien practice, he still preferred old-fashioned soap and water.

"Let me get straight to the point," Nog said, kneeling down next to the turtle-necked alien.

"Please do," Forsh answered. "Your uncle Quark has quite a reputation. I suspect that his young nephew may have an offer worth hearing."

"It's the alien creature—"

"The one that the spacer Darm tried to sell me," Forsh interrupted, "but forgot to mention that he did not own."

"Yes. The creature, Babe, belongs to us." Nog indicated that Jake was his partner in this potential deal.

"And you wish to sell him?"

"If the price is to our liking, we would consider such a transaction."

Jake bit his tongue. *What was Nog agreeing to do?*

Forsh leaned back in the mud. His tongue flicked out and snagged an unwary whisper fly that had ventured too close. "The little creature would make a welcome addition to my collection."

Forsh turned his head and gave Nog a hard look. "I

will not haggle," he told him, "but the price would be to your liking. That I guarantee. When can you make the delivery?"

Nog rose to his feet. "Tomorrow evening—if we decide to sell."

"I look forward to your decision. I trust it will benefit both of us." Forsh leaned even farther back and submerged himself completely into the muck.

When they were outside the spa, Jake asked Nog, "What was that all about?"

"If Darm had stolen Babe, he would have already made a deal. Forsh wouldn't be interested in us."

"Maybe he isn't. Maybe he just wants us to think he is so we don't get suspicious."

"Maybe. But I don't think so. Ferengi have an ear for negotiations. Forsh definitely wants to make a deal."

"Then Darm doesn't have Babe."

"Not yet."

Jake thought about it, then wondered aloud, "If Babe was scared, he'd probably go back to where he came from."

"But," Nog argued, "how would he get back to the Gamma Quadrant?"

"No. I don't mean his home planet. I mean the starship that brought him through the wormhole—the *Ulysses.*"

They found the *Ulysses* in docking bay two, which was in the oldest area of the station. The air in the corridor that led to the airlock was musty with the stale smells from a thousand starships that had anchored here when Deep Space Nine was still a Cardassian mining station.

Jake thought the odors gave the place a mood of romance and adventure. Nog complained that it simply stank.

Captain Pavlov was in his cabin going over the cargo manifests on his compupad. In contrast to the spit and polish of a Starfleet vessel, the *Ulysses* was old and pitted with age. The captain's quarters were even more cramped than Jake had expected.

"Life in the merchant fleet is quite different from being on one of your father's starships," Pavlov remarked as he read Jake's expression.

"I didn't mean—" Jake started to explain.

Pavlov brushed the air with his hand, as though cleaning away invisible cobwebs. "Don't apologize. The *Ulysses* is old and probably should be retired. We both should be." He tugged at his red beard. "But neither of us would last long if we weren't roaming the spaceways."

Pavlov leaned back in his chair, which creaked under his shifting weight. "But what can an old space dog do for you young lads?"

Jake told him about the disappearance of Babe.

The captain listened patiently, then spoke. "I doubt that the creature would return here. I'm sure his time with Darm was not pleasant."

"But if he's frightened, this is a familiar place," Nog said.

"Aye. There is that."

52

Captain Pavlov swiveled in his chair and punched a code into the wall computer. Jake was startled that he didn't speak to the computer like everyone else did.

"I hate machines that talk. I'm old-fashioned that way," Pavlov commented while he read the display. "Since we're under Federation contract, I have to maintain a log of everyone and everything that comes on or goes off the *Ulysses.*" He paused while the data continued to scroll on the screen. "Your creature didn't come back here to hide. There would be a record in the computer."

"He couldn't have sneaked aboard?" Nog asked.

"Or been smuggled on?" Jake added, thinking of Darm.

Pavlov shook his head. "No. Since we spoke in the commander's office, I turned up security a notch or two. Anything coming aboard the *Ulysses* is now logged automatically." He switched off the display and turned his attention back to Jake and Nog. "Sorry, lads. You'll have to look somewhere else for your pet."

But where? Jake wondered.

"Shouldn't you be doing your homework?" Commander Sisko asked his son as Jake and Nog entered Operations. It was suppertime and the normally hectic nerve center of Deep Space Nine was almost empty. Only Vork, the Bajoran maintenance trainee who was currently assigned to Chief O'Brien, was there running some tests at the engineering console. Major Kira was

DEEP SPACE NINE

seated across from Sisko at the Operations Table, where they had been writing some of the monthly Starfleet status reports that the commander dreaded.

"Babe's missing," Jake told his father.

"Odo informed me. But I thought you two detectives would have found him by now."

Jake shook his head. "We've looked everywhere."

"Maybe he went back to the *Ulysses,*" Kira suggested.

"No," Nog replied. "We asked Captain Pavlov. He hasn't seen him."

"I'm sure he'll show up," Sisko said.

Jake understood his father was trying to be sympathetic, but he had already formed a close attachment to the alien creature in the short period they had been together. He wanted his father to do something.

"Can't you scan for him?" Jake asked as he stepped up to the Operations Table.

"If he were wearing a communicator. But otherwise there's no way for the computer to locate your pet."

"Can't you have Odo's men search for him?"

"Odo is busy with these strange apparitions."

"Apparitions?" Nog asked.

"He means ghosts," Jake told Nog.

"The visual hallucinations that have been popping up on the Promenade," Kira explained. "They're driving Odo crazy."

"They're beginning to have the same effect on me," Sisko said.

Jake knew that his father was uncomfortable with anything he couldn't explain in rational terms. Another

54

time and Jake would have wanted to be involved in solving the mystery. But now he had a more urgent need. They just had to find Babe.

Kira studied the faces of the two boys. "Couldn't we post a description of Babe throughout the station?" she suggested, looking up at the commander. "Anyone who sees him report to Operations?"

The idea seemed reasonable enough to Jake.

"Do it," Sisko told Kira, obviously agreeing.

But before the Bajoran major could enter the information into her computer terminal, she was interrupted by a beep.

"Something coming through the wormhole," Kira said as she analyzed the readout that was displayed on the Operations Table.

"What do you mean, *something?*" Sisko asked.

"I'm not sure."

"Not sure of what?" Sisko stepped up next to Kira to see the readout for himself.

"If it's a ship," Kira said in disbelief, "it's big. *Very* big."

"Put it on the viewer. Let's get a look at our visitor," Sisko ordered.

Major Kira ran her fingers over the control console. "Viewer on."

The large overhead screen switched on and displayed a three-dimensional view of the Bajoran star system. Because the image was a hologram, the same perspective was visible to everyone in Ops.

"Magnify. Let's see the wormhole."

The image of the Denorios asteroid belt expanded. The screens still showed nothing but the empty starscape.

"Where is it?" Sisko asked.

Kira looked down at her control screen. "It should be visible—now!"

The wormhole suddenly blinked into existence. It was like some cosmic eye that opened as it awoke. The familiar multicolored tunnel spiraled out of the black void.

Then the ship came through the wormhole.

It was *big*.

It was *very* big.

Jake had seen a lot of starships come through the wormhole. But never anything *that* big.

Nog's mouth dropped open in amazement.

Kira finally broke the silence. "I didn't think anything that big could get through the wormhole in one piece."

"I'd agree with you, Major," Sisko said. "Except for the evidence on our screen."

It was a starship. Jake could see that. But it was not like any starship he had ever seen before. It was a sphere and it pulsated with strange, hypnotic colors. It reminded Jake of a big soap bubble. But the way the colors throbbed, this bubble seemed to be almost alive.

Behind the strange starship the wormhole closed. Once again there was only empty space. Except now the giant sphere blotted out the starfields and everything else. It filled the holographic screen with its gigantic presence.

And it was coming straight toward them.

CHAPTER 6

For a long moment no one in Operations moved. It was as if they were part of a holosuite drama and the program had been frozen, except that this drama was all too real. Jake noted that for once even Nog was speechless.

The giant sphere that had come out of the wormhole continued on a collision course with Deep Space Nine.

Sisko was the first to react to the potential danger. "Shields up," he called.

Kira quickly punched the necessary codes into the Ops terminal. "Defensive shields raised."

"Protection will not be necessary. For the moment." The voice boomed out of nowhere, exploding in their ears.

All eyes turned to the main viewscreen. The spherical starship had stopped and hung in a threatening position uncomfortably close to the station. Now that image was replaced by a face.

Or was it a face?

Jake had never seen anything quite like it. Where he expected to see the being's head, Jake saw a much smaller version of the throbbing energy bubble that had come through the wormhole.

Again the voice boomed in their ears. *"I am Oryx. Admiral of the High Command. Defender of the Truth. Protector of the Faith. Guardian of the Line."*

There was another long moment, then Jake saw his father take a deliberate step forward so that attention would be focused on him.

"I am Benjamin Sisko. Commander of Deep Space Nine. How can we help you?"

"By returning that whom you have abducted."

"I do not understand. Who is it you think we have abducted?"

"The Next in Line."

"What is the 'Next in Line'?"

"It is he. The one who would be the next to rule our world."

"I don't know if whoever you're looking for is here on our station. But you are welcome to search."

A gloved hand reached up and lifted the energy bubble to reveal a face that was almost human, though it was purple, and lizardlike, and framed by ragged flaps of thick pebbled skin. The glove and uniform seemed spun from some metallic material.

"You try my patience, Commander Sisko." The voice that spoke was no longer booming, but the threat was still present. Very much present.

"I don't mean to, Admiral. But you arrive here without warning and accuse us of stealing something—or someone—whom you seem unable or unwilling to describe."

"We know the prince is among you."

"Exactly *how* do you know that?"

"One of the ships to which you have given protection carried the prince to your station."

"Which ship?"

"That we do not know. But we know the ship passed through the hole in space ahead of us."

"Dozens of ships came through the wormhole in the past two days for the celebration. It could be any of them. Or it could be none of them."

"One of those ships stole our prince," the Admiral maintained.

"But you don't know which one?"

"We do not have that information."

Sisko's frustration was echoed in his words. "If you can't tell us which ship you suspect, then I would ask you to display a picture of your missing prince."

The admiral seemed to take that suggestion as an insult. "Do you know what you ask?"

"Only for a picture. How can we find your prince if we don't know what he looks like?"

"It is impossible. In his present state it is forbidden for any to look upon His Royal Highness. He was nearing the end of his Solitary when he was abducted."

"What is Solitary?"

"That is our business and does not concern you."

"It does if you want our help."

"You continue to try my patience, Commander." The gloved hand reached for a switch. "I allow you one day of your time in which to return that which is ours."

"And if we fail to find your prince?"

"Then we have no other choice under our law." The admiral replaced his helmet. *"We will destroy your station."*

"And risk destroying your prince along with it?"

"If it must be done, it will be done. If the prince cannot be returned to us, he must perish with those who have taken him. It is our law."

"What kind of law is it that would punish hundreds of innocent people because someone you seek *might* be on this station?"

"It is not for you to understand our laws. It is sufficient that you know it is *our law—and it will be carried out if you do not find and deliver our prince."*

The screen went blank.

Jake squirmed. His father was smart. He might even be the smartest man on Deep Space Nine. But how could anyone find someone when they didn't know what he looked like?

Twenty minutes later the increased activity in Operations reminded Jake of a Ntok ant colony under siege. The off-duty crew members had been summoned back and now busily studied the logs of all ships that had come through the wormhole in the past three weeks. Jake watched them search through the databases for any clue that might point to the missing prince. The task seemed hopeless since no one had any idea what they were looking for.

In another part of the room, Deep Space Nine's senior staff gathered around the Operations Table. Besides Commander Sisko and Major Kira, they included Engineering Chief Miles O'Brien; Science Officer Jadzia Dax; Medical Officer Julian Bashir; and the station's security chief, Odo.

"That's what we're up against." Sisko concluded his summary of the events of the past hour. "Any thoughts?"

"Have you tried to reestablish contact with the alien ship?" Dax asked.

Kira nodded. "They won't respond."

Sisko looked at O'Brien. "Chief, if it comes down to hostilities, can this station defend itself against their attack?"

O'Brien considered this for a long moment. The chief was not a man to rush to conclusions. Finally he replied. "Unknown, Commander. That's a Borg-size warship hanging over our heads. I have to believe their weapons are pretty powerful."

Jake saw the momentary grimace on his father's face at the mention of the Borg. He felt the same flash of anger and sorrow as he remembered the battle at Wolf 359 and the death of his mother at the hands of the Borg.

"That's bad," Julian Bashir said, voicing his concern.

"Very bad," O'Brien continued. "To put it in simple

terms, we'd be like a duck in a shooting gallery if it comes to a fight."

"Then we must ensure that it does not come to that," Sisko said.

"All they seem to want," said Kira, "is the return of their prince."

"Unfortunately," Odo spoke up, "there is no record of anyone matching the description of the alien on the ship arriving on the station. We don't even know if that is what their prince looks like."

"He must be here," Bashir said.

"Not necessarily, Doctor," Odo explained patiently. "Just because these aliens think he came through the wormhole does not make it a fact."

"But they believe it, Constable." Sisko stood up from the table. He instinctively paced whenever faced with a difficult dilemma. "And as long they think we have their prince, that's all that matters."

Sisko stopped and faced his staff. "I'm open to suggestions."

No one spoke. Then there was a cough from the background.

Jake and Nog had been sitting quietly in a corner during all this. Now Jake cautiously took a step forward.

"Jake." Sisko looked at his son. "You shouldn't be here."

"Ah, Dad—you asked for suggestions."

"That's right, Benjamin," Dax reminded him. "You did ask."

"Right. So what do you suggest, Jake?"

Jake hesitated a moment. He hadn't quite thought it all through. "If you know where the alien ship came from, then you could check the logs of the ships docked here to see which of them was in their star system."

"But we don't know where the aliens came from."

"Couldn't you ask them?"

Commander Sisko took his son's advice and ordered Major Kira to send a message to the alien ship.

There was no verbal reply, but almost instantly a data transmission was received by Deep Space Nine's computer system.

Dax stepped to her console and studied the input. "I think they've given us what we asked for."

"You think?"

"Their star charts are quite different from ours. And since we have no extensive maps of the Gamma Quadrant, it is going to take some time to translate their data into something we can understand."

"Time is something we don't have a lot of, Dax."

"I realize that, Benjamin."

"Do the best you can—as fast as you can." Sisko turned to Odo. "Constable, I want you to start an immediate full-scale search of the station. You have to assume that if the prince is here, he is either avoiding us or being held captive."

Odo rose from the Operations Table. "If their missing prince is anywhere on Deep Space Nine, I'll find him."

Sisko turned to Chief O'Brien. "Go with him, Chief.

You know the ins and outs of this station better than anyone."

O'Brien quickly rose and followed Odo to the turbolift, while the others quickly went to their control stations.

Jake nudged Nog. "We're not going to be much help in finding the prince. My dad can take care of that. We need to find our missing pet."

Odo did not expect that finding a missing prince or a lost pet on Deep Space Nine would be difficult. There were not many places on the station where someone could hide or be hidden. At least, that was what Odo had thought when he and O'Brien started searching for the prince. But by the following morning he had not found a single clue that pointed to the possible whereabouts of the prince.

"I don't think he's here," Odo confided to O'Brien as they walked through one of the connecting tunnels that linked the habitat ring to the docking ring. "We've searched all the guest quarters."

"We've tried the obvious. Maybe it's time to try the *un*obvious." O'Brien was busy looking at the station blueprints on his palm computer.

"If you have an idea, Chief, don't keep it to yourself."

"Well," O'Brien mumbled as he punched keys, "these are the original Cardassian diagrams." He hit another key, and the display changed to include another set of diagrams that overlaid the first. They were in different colors, so any differences were apparent. "And this is the way it looks today."

Odo studied the display, then pointed a finger and asked a question. "What goes on in these places where only the old structures exist?"

"These areas were sealed off. We don't use them."

"But is there access to them?"

"To some of them, I'm sure there is. Others are probably blocked by solid bermite plates. Stronger than steel or titanium. No one could get into them."

"We'll have a look, just in case someone did find a way in."

"But how—?"

How required O'Brien to slice through the solid metal of the old plates.

It was cramped inside the abandoned power conduit, and O'Brien was sweating from the heat generated by the laser drill. The air was stale, and the lack of environmental controls in this section made the task all the more miserable. Fortunately it was the last of the sealed-off areas they had to search. But it was also proving to be the most difficult to penetrate.

"It's going to take another twenty minutes to cut an opening big enough to get through," he told Odo.

Odo agreed with O'Brien that this was most likely a fool's errand; nevertheless he had to follow up any possibility. The constable stepped past O'Brien and stood in front of the narrow slot that the Operations chief had just pierced through the bermite.

"It's big enough now," Odo said.

While O'Brien watched with fascination, Odo poured himself into a thin snakelike form, not unlike the modeling plastic that his daughter, Molly, played with. Quickly the form that Odo had become vanished through the slot in the wall.

For a minute or two that seemed to last much longer, O'Brien waited. Then the snake flowed back out of the slot onto the floor of the conduit and reformed back into the more familiar form of the station constable.

"Nothing is inside there," Odo pronounced when he was back to his old shape.

"I'd love to be able to do what you can do," O'Brien said eagerly. "Then I'd really be able to get into my work."

"As you humans say, 'The grass is always greener in the other posture.' "

"It's 'pasture,' " corrected O'Brien. "But you're right. Most of us want to be what we aren't."

"And what we aren't at the moment is finding the lost prince. Where do you suggest we look next?"

O'Brien looked at the display on his palm computer. "Beats me. We've looked everywhere the blueprints suggest. But there may be other hidden nooks and crannies on the station that the Cardassians didn't bother to put into their blueprints. Finding them could take a long time."

"Time is the one commodity we are rapidly running out of," Odo warned.

* * *

Jake and Nog, who were engaged in their own search elsewhere on the station, were also aware that time was running out.

It was the middle of the morning, and they had found no trace of their missing pet.

"I'm running out of places to look," Nog said wearily as they sat on the balcony, their feet dangling above the crowded Promenade. No one except the Operations team and Odo's security guards were aware of the threat from the enormous ship.

Jake was not even thinking about the aliens aboard the ship. He was lost in thought, remembering an old story, a mystery in which the object that everyone was looking for was never found *because it was "hidden" in plain sight.*

"There's one place we forgot to look," Jake said suddenly as he leaped to his feet.

"Where's that?"

"The obvious place. The one place on this station where Babe might feel safe."

"Our clubhouse!" Nog shouted as he followed Jake at a fast run.

CHAPTER 7

Meanwhile, in Operations, Benjamin Sisko saw that his people were running out of options.

"Okay, everyone," he said. "Let's stop and put together what we have."

"What we have is less than four hours," Major Kira reminded him, though it was apparent from their actions that no one in the room needed to be reminded of that fact.

"We've had no luck finding their prince," O'Brien said. "Odo's still searching, but it's pretty clear that he isn't here."

"Try to contact the alien ship," Sisko told Dax.

The Trill science officer swiveled her chair and keyed in a command at her terminal.

"They don't want to talk to us," Dax said after trying for a few minutes with no results.

"They must," Sisko said. He pounded his fist on the

Operations Table with a show of emotion that was unlike his normal tightly controlled composure.

"We are listening." The voice echoed throughout the room.

Everyone turned to the main screen. The image was of the huge alien ship that hung near Deep Space Nine. It was, Sisko thought, dangling there like a bomb. He hoped that the bomb was not primed.

"We have searched for your prince," Sisko said, "but he is not on this station."

Now the ship in the viewer was replaced by the energy helmet of the alien admiral.

"We know that he is there," came the voice.

"Then, unless you want a war, help us."

"What help do you seek?"

"Beam down a boarding party from your ship to help us in the search."

"That is not possible."

"Then what is possible?" Sisko snapped, the anger apparent in his voice. "Without some cooperation on your part, you make it impossible to find your prince."

"We have sent our star maps to your computer. That is enough. Find the ship that trespassed against us, and make those responsible return our prince."

"We have not yet been able to coordinate your view of the Gamma Quadrant with our own charts. We need time."

"You have three of the time units that you call hours."

"But—"

"That is all the time you have. This contact is terminated. Now."

The energy helmet on the viewer vanished, to be replaced once more by the alien ship.

Sisko turned to his science officer. "Dax, how much do we know?"

Dax studied her terminal. "Their world is named Pyx. That's about it."

"But which of the starships in our docking bays was in their system?"

"That I don't know, Benjamin."

"How long before you will know?"

Dax punched in a code, read the results. "Ninety minutes and I should have an answer."

"That's cuttin' it awful close, Commander," O'Brien observed.

"Too close, Chief," Sisko replied. "But it will have to be good enough."

At the same time, in the upper pylon, Jake and Nog found Babe precisely where Jake had predicted. The little alien creature was asleep on a shelf in their clubhouse.

"Babe!" Jake yelled as he ran over and hugged his furry friend.

Babe stirred sleepily and nuzzled Jake with his soft horn.

"He seems tired," Nog declared.

Jake had noticed it, too. "Maybe he's hungry," he said, while continuing to stroke the thick fur.

Nog stepped over to the old replicator he had borrowed from storage. They hadn't used it in more than a month, not since the disaster when Nog had tried to prepare his grandmother's acclaimed Ferengi swamp salad, apparently overtaxing the machine's faltering microcircuits. Since then the results of any request were unpredictable.

"This isn't going to work," Nog announced after a few abortive attempts to produce something simple and edible.

Their only choice was to go down to Quark's and select a range of potential foods that might fit Babe's diet. Since they had no idea what the little creature thrived on, they would have to bring up a little bit of everything.

"We really should see Dr. Bashir first," Jake said as they prepared to leave. Babe was still resting on the shelf, and Jake was concerned.

"He's too busy with the search for the missing prince," Nog replied. "Besides, Babe is smart enough that he'll only pick those foods that are good for him."

"I guess we really don't have much choice," Jake rationalized as he followed Nog out the door.

Left alone again in the clubhouse, Babe slept fitfully.

Suddenly he bolted awake. There was the sound of footsteps approaching heavily.

Darm appeared in the doorway, wearing an angry grin that was even more menacing than his scar. "Well, now, what have we here?" He blocked the exit with his body.

"I thought following those brats might lead me to you."

Babe leaped from his shelf to the center of the room to face his enemy.

"This time you're not getting away," Darm said threateningly. He took a phaser out from under his tunic. "And this is to make sure you don't."

CHAPTER 8

Jake and Nog returned in time to see it happen—but not in time to prevent it from happening.

They had reached the doorway to their clubhouse, arms loaded with cartons of food to tempt Babe, when they saw Darm. They saw him raise his phaser and take deliberate aim. And they watched helplessly as he fired a single low-energy blast that struck Babe in the chest. The furry little creature whimpered, trying to fight off the paralysis. He fell on his side and lay on the floor twitching.

Darm adjusted the phaser's control. "Looks like you need a stronger dose. I don't want you waking up before I hand you over to Forsh."

"No!" Jake and Nog shouted together. They dropped their food cartons and charged at Darm. Both boys together were no match for the much stronger third officer of the *Ulysses,* but the unexpectedness of their

attack caught Darm off balance. He fell to the deck, and his phaser flew from his grasp.

Darm roared like a wounded lion. He struggled to his feet. "You laddies are in trouble—*deep* trouble." He came for Jake first.

Jake rolled, avoiding the spacer's initial rush. "Get the phaser!" Jake yelled to Nog as he scrambled toward the door.

Darm was already on his way to retrieve the phaser, but Nog leaped at the spacer and attempted to tackle the much bigger man around the legs. That slowed Darm down for a moment, and if anything, it made him even angrier.

Darm reached out and grabbed Nog by the arm. Nog howled in that particular way that Ferengi do when in trouble. Darm ignored Nog's yell and lifted the boy high into the air. But he did not have a chance to do anything else, because Jake splashed a bowl of Cayon chili into the spacer's face. It was only warm, but the thick glop momentarily covered Darm's eyes.

"I can't see!" he screamed.

Jake seized the opportunity to dodge past and scoop up the phaser. "Hands up," Jake ordered, trying to imitate his father's authoritative voice.

Darm scraped the chili from his eyes with his right hand while continuing to hold the struggling Nog with his left.

"Put the phaser down," Darm snarled.

Jake took a step backward. He wasn't sure what stun level the controls were set for, and he certainly didn't want to hit Nog.

Darm used Jake's moment of hesitation to snake his brawny arm around Nog's neck. Nog howled even louder.

"Put the phaser down, or I break your Ferengi friend's neck." Darm twisted his arm tighter, and Nog's howl was cut off by a choking sound.

Jake hesitated another moment.

It was all the time an experienced street fighter like Darm needed. He threw Nog at Jake.

Both boys tumbled against the wall. Jake held onto the phaser—but not for long. Darm stepped over and forced his heavy boot against Jake's arm. Then he reached down and ripped the phaser out of Jake's weakening grasp. Darm stepped backward, releasing Jake.

The two boys huddled together against the wall.

Darm slowly raised the phaser. "You lads have caused me plenty of grief." He gave them a twisted smile. "It's payback time."

Darm aimed the deadly phaser. But he never had a chance to fire the weapon, because at that moment the roof fell in on him—literally.

Jake and Nog watched in amazement as the ceiling of the construction shed collapsed on top of the spacer. Darm let out a scream and ran out, saving himself, and making no attempt to rescue Jake, Nog, or Babe.

But, strange as it seemed, they had no need to be rescued. For as soon as Darm was gone, the destruction vanished. The room was back the way it had been before the cave-in.

"What happened?" Nog wanted to know.

Jake looked over at Babe. "It's Babe."

"What?"

"He did it. Babe created some kind of hypnotic illusion." Babe crossed over and laid his head in Jake's lap.

"Then it was Babe who caused the illusions in the Promenade," Nog reasoned.

"Yes," Jake agreed. "It must be the way he defends himself in the wild. A kind of camouflage."

Jake stroked the golden fur on Babe's horn. The little creature sighed. He appeared to be exhausted, as though the effort of saving them had drained all his energy.

"Take it easy, Babe." Jake tried to comfort his pet. "The bad man is gone."

Suddenly Babe began to shake, as if he had been zapped by a lightning bolt. He rolled off of Jake's lap and shivered uncontrollably on the floor.

Jake and Nog watched Babe's seizures, helpless to do anything. Finally the convulsions subsided. Babe struggled weakly to his feet.

"Easy, Babe." Jake tried to sound reassuring as he stepped forward, but his insides were twisting as if he had swallowed a Gobian spit worm. Something strange was happening to his friend, and he had absolutely no idea of how to stop it. Before Jake could reach Babe, the creature shuddered again. Then he turned and bolted for the door. "Nog, catch him!" Jake yelled.

Nog tried to intercept the little rhino, but he leaped and missed. Babe dashed past and was out the door. Ferengi might be financial wheeler-dealers, but athletes they definitely were not.

Jake thought fast, trying to imagine what his father would do in this situation. Something was wrong with Babe, and the creature needed help from an expert. "You go get Dr. Bashir," Jake told Nog. "I'll find Babe."

Nog hurried out of the room without his usual argument.

Jake knew that when it came down to the crunch, Nog trusted his judgment—at least when there was no profit potential involved. But now he had to do his part and find Babe. Only he didn't know where to start looking. Then Jake remembered that Babe had originally sought the highest shelf in the clubhouse, and he reasoned that the injured creature might again seek the high ground.

Jake went to the end of the short corridor outside their clubhouse and began to climb the ladder toward the top of the docking pylon.

This section of Deep Space Nine had never really been finished—at least on the inside. A framework of beams intertwined with loose cabling. The abandoned tube stretched upward and curved slightly inward as it narrowed near the top.

Occasionally small work platforms gave Jake something solid on which to rest. He glanced over the edge and saw it was a long way down to the bottom of the pylon. A very long way.

"Babe," Jake called out nervously. "Where are you?" This wasn't going exactly as he hoped. If there was one thing that Jake really disliked it was high places.

Jake took another step upon the ladder. Suddenly a rusted rung broke under his weight. Frantically Jake reached out for something to hold on to—but the top half of the ladder pulled away from the frame. Jake was left dangling from the broken ladder in the center of the tube—high above the base of the pylon.

Slowly the bolts that anchored the bottom section of the ladder began to loosen.

Jake closed his eyes and, to make himself stop shaking, concentrated on what he had to do next. Only he didn't know what to do next. He wished that his father were there.

Things weren't going much better in Operations. Sisko watched impatiently as his engineering chief attempted to repair an unanticipated problem in the main computer's logic memory.

"Blasted Caradassian technology," O'Brien muttered under his breath.

"I don't care who's responsible, Chief. Fix it!"

"I'm doing my best, Commander." O'Brien was about to try replacing his fifth circuit board. This one had better be it. The time limit the Pyxians had given them was about to run out. And they still hadn't figured out which of the ships in dock had visited the alien's star system. With all the extra traffic from the wormhole celebration, their job wasn't made any easier.

"Chief, if you please," Dax's soft voice cajoled.

O'Brien slid the board into place and made sure it was tight. "Okay, try it now."

Dax pushed a few keys. After a microsecond of hesitation, a star map of the Gamma Quadrant appeared on her screen. This was a partial view of a Starfleet survey map of the systems nearest the wormhole. Now she pushed another button, and the first starmap was overlaid by a second map which contained many more stars. This was the translated data from the Pyxians. "We've got a ninety-nine percent match," she told Sisko, the relief evident in her voice.

"Put it on the main screen," Sisko ordered.

Instantly a holographic image of the Gamma Quadrant materialized on the main viewscreen.

"Computer, which one is the Pyxian system?" asked Major Kira.

One star in the image began to blink.

"Computer, magnify."

At Kira's command the screen zoomed in on the blinking star, exploding it into an image of a star system with eleven planets and twenty-four moons.

"Okay, we know where they came from," Sisko observed. "Now, who's been there?"

"Computer, match Pyxian system to captain's logs of starships now docked at Deep Space Nine."

"One match found," the voice of the computer responded.

"Computer, show us the match," Sisko commanded.

Immediately the silhouette of a starship was overlaid on the holographic image of the star system. "The matching ship is the Federation exploration vessel *Ulysses.*"

"I should have guessed," Odo muttered as he ran for the turbolift. "I'll have your missing prince—or know exactly what happened to him—in ten minutes," he said as the lift doors closed behind him.

"Kira, contact the Pyxians," Sisko ordered. "Let's see if we can keep things from getting out of hand until Odo gets back."

"I'm trying," Kira replied as her fingers played over the control panel. "But there's a lot of static. It's almost as if—"

Kira's words stopped in mid-sentence.

So did everything else.

A low rumble seemed to come from somewhere beneath their feet. If they had been on a planet it might have come from the bowels of the earth. It was like an—

"Earthquake!" An ensign shouted instinctively, leaping for cover under a table and ignoring the absurdity of his statement.

Suddenly the room vibrated violently. People and objects were tossed about as if they were toys in a dollhouse that was being shaken by a giant child. One of the auxiliary computers broke loose and flew across the room, narrowly missing Kira. The cable holding an overhead monitor snapped, and the viewer fell and smashed on top of the Operations Table.

The room continued shaking as people hurried to find shelter.

"It's the Pyxians!" someone shouted.

"Our grace period just ran out," Dax said.

The attack had begun.

CHAPTER 9

Jake did not feel the rumbling that was happening elsewhere on Deep Space Nine. At the moment, hanging from a broken ladder high above nothing in the upper pylon shaft, he had more immediate concerns on his mind.

Cautiously he stretched out his right hand, while continuing to hold tight to the ladder rung with his left. He fingers brushed against thin air. The safety of the wall beams was beyond his reach. The shaft disappeared into the dimness, seemingly miles below.

He tried extending his arm farther. The ladder creaked as he shifted his weight. The bolts holding the bottom section to the wall groaned. One of them snapped. *What would Dad do?*

Jake wondered whether his father had ever been in a situation like this one. He knew a senior officer of a Starfleet ship had plenty of opportunities to face death. That was the kind of opportunity that Jake would have been glad to forgo—indefinitely. But here it was, and he had to do something. *Now.*

If he continued to hang here, his arms would eventually get tired, and he'd fall. Or the bolts would break or loosen from the wall, and the ladder would fall, taking him with it.

There was one chance. He could make one big swing that would carry him across the abyss to the far wall—and safety. But he would have only one try. The effort would almost certainly pull the bolts loose from their tenuous moorings, plunging the ladder into the shaft. And if he couldn't grab on to something solid on the far wall, he'd be right behind it.

After an instant of hesitation, he made his decision.

Jake closed his eyes and swung his body backward. He heard the bolts grind as they tore free of the wall. Then he opened his eyes and swung forward, letting go of the ladder rung when he reached the top of his arc. Like an acrobat on a trapeze, Jake flew across the empty void.

For one long moment he was sure he wasn't going to make it. Then his hand grabbed on to a beam, and he pulled himself tight against the wall.

Behind him the ladder broke free and dropped down into the dark void of the shaft, clanging again and again off the sides as it fell.

Jake held tight to the beam for several minutes, shaking as he thought about what might have happened if he had missed. Soon the shaking subsided. He had made it. He was safe.

THE PET

Very slowly and very carefully Jake began to descend from the upper shaft of the pylon.

He was almost back to the clubhouse level when he remembered why he was here.

Where was Babe?

Elsewhere Deep Space Nine was experiencing utter chaos. The Promenade was rapidly becoming a disaster zone. People fled as huge steel girders surged up through the floor of the mall like metallic prehistoric monsters. One girder shot skyward like an arrow and anchored itself in the ceiling, dangling precariously over the heads of fleeing pedestrians.

One section of the balcony overlooking the Promenade split apart. Only the quick reaction of one of the assistant engineers prevented several Bajoran sightseers from plunging through the crevice.

Rolling shock waves shook the station like an endless series of earthquakes and sent anything not tied down— and quite a bit that was—careening across the open spaces. An alert security guard scooped up a child who had stumbled and was about to be rolled over by a runaway maintenance cart and hustled her to safety.

People ducked and dodged objects coming at them from every direction. The Promenade had become a live mine field, and no place seemed safe. But incredibly, in spite of the panic and the property damage, no one was injured by any of these flying projectiles.

Quark watched in dismay as his entire stock of vintage

Juno wines tumbled off the shelves, ending up in a pool of pink liquid at his feet. With his establishment collapsing around him, Quark took the only prudent course of action open to him—he hid under the bar.

"Some security," Quark cursed as yet another shelf of expensive spirits crashed down on him. "Odo, where are you when I need you?"

Meanwhile, in Operations, Commander Sisko was asking the same question. "Where is Odo?"

"He was on his way to the docking bay where the *Ulysses* is berthed," Kira replied. "But I can't seem to get a fix on his communicator badge. I can't get a fix on anyone's comm badge."

Another quake shook Ops. Anything that wasn't secured again flew across the room. The whole station seemed to be coming apart at the seams.

"What're the Pyxians hitting us with?" Sisko asked, holding on to the sides of the Operations Table.

"Unknown," Kira replied, trying to work her computer terminal. "Appears to be some kind of high-frequency blasts. They're tearing the station apart."

"That's obvious! But what do we do about it?"

"Fire has broken out in docking bay two," Dax reported.

"Send an emergency team," Sisko responded.

"I don't have an emergency team to send," O'Brien countered. "Right now everyone I have is in at least three places at once."

"Can't you contact the Pyxians?" Sisko appealed to Kira.

"I'm sending, Commander. But if they're receiving, they're not telling me about it."

At that moment the largest quake yet struck the station.

We can't take this much longer, Sisko thought. *Odo, you better come up with something fast.*

With the station coming apart, Darm struggled back toward where the runabouts were docked. Under the circumstances, with the docking bays in chaos, a large ship had no chance to escape, but a smaller runabout might sneak away in the confusion. Darm did not mind deserting a sinking ship, even if he had to leave everyone else behind.

Maybe not everyone. For it was at that moment that Darm saw Babe. The furry little alien creature was sitting in the middle of the corridor, almost as if he were waiting for the spacer. Darm took it as a sign that his luck was finally changing for the good. He smiled.

"Gotcha," Darm said as he grabbed Babe.

Surprisingly the creature made no attempt to escape.

"At least I'll leave this cursed place with a few bars of gold-pressed latinum in my pockets." Darm whistled as he carried the creature down the corridor.

Darm found the alien Forsh near the airlock to his ship. None of the airlocks was functioning, so there was no way to get aboard.

90

"Even if there were a way, nothing is leaving the station," wailed Forsh. "We're all doomed!"

"Then you won't mind paying me for delivering this," Darm said as he shoved Babe forward.

"What am I going to do with that thing when this whole station is falling apart?"

"Frankly, I don't really care," was Darm's hard response. "But we made a deal. And you're going to honor it." Darm took out his phaser to emphasize the point.

While nodding, Forsh took something from his belt pouch. It was a slender card that resembled a computer microcircuit board. It was actually a bearer note that could be exchanged for five bars of gold-pressed latinum, with no questions asked, anywhere in the Federation. "This is the amount we agreed upon," Forsh said as he handed the card to Darm.

Darm took the card, then reached into Forsh's belt pouch and removed four more of the cards. "I've just upped the price."

When the alien tried to stop him, Darm shoved him back and raised the phaser threateningly. "Any complaints?"

Forsh looked at the phaser and at the harsh expression on Darm's face.

Another quake hit the station.

Forsh stumbled against the wall. "Take what you want," he told Darm wearily. "Just go and leave me."

Darm started to exit, then stopped. He looked down at Babe, who had been sitting nearby during all this. "He's all yours, Forsh."

Suddenly the fuzzy creature rose up on his hind legs. Except it wasn't the creature that was rising. It was something else.

Babe was becoming *Odo*.

"You! The shapeshifting sheriff!" Darm roared.

The metamorphosis was complete, and Odo was once more his humanoid self. "Security Chief is the proper title." Odo took a step forward. "You are under arrest."

Darm focused the phaser on him. "You got no charges."

"Selling something you don't own is a start."

Darm looked around. "There's nothing here that I tried to sell." Which was perfectly true, since Babe had been replaced by Odo.

"The real charge," Odo explained, "is abduction of the Pyxian prince."

"What prince? I don't know what you're talkin' about."

"I've just checked the logs of the *Ulysses*. It did enter the star system of the Pyxians. You were on one of their moons."

"So. I didn't take no prince."

"I believe you did," Odo asserted.

"Then where is he?"

"That is what you are going to tell me."

Darm raised the phaser. "I'm tellin' you nothing, lawman." The spacer fired at Odo at point-blank range.

The beam hit Odo full in the chest. Then the beam did a remarkable thing. It bounced off his chest and ricocheted back at Darm. The reflected beam struck the

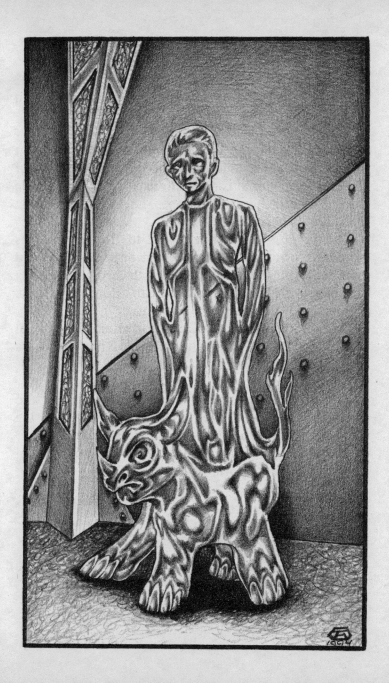

spacer and doubled him over as though he had been hammered by a fist.

Forsh watched all this with amazement.

Odo smiled. He tapped his bulked-up chest. "It's what old Earth lawmen used to call a 'bulletproof vest.' Of course, this material is much more efficient. And elastic enough to stretch into any shape," he added as his chest assumed its normal size.

The Security Chief knelt next to the unconscious spacer. "Fortunately, the reflected blast only stunned him. Unfortunately, that is enough to keep him sleeping for quite a while. Which means I can't discover what he knows about the prince for some time."

Odo returned the cards Darm had attempted to steal from Forsh. "I suggest in the future you find yourself a more reputable business associate."

Another quake rumbled through the station.

Odo grabbed the unconscious Darm by the collar and dragged him toward the turbolifts. Around him the station seemed to be on the verge of disintegrating.

"Of course," Odo remarked, "at the moment none of us seems to have a future to speak of."

CHAPTER 10

Jake was also worried about his future. He had searched most of the upper sections of the pylon and found no trace of Babe. He feared that the alien, like other sick or injured creatures, might have crawled into some hole for security. In such cases the animal usually died because no one was there to help him. Jake did not want that to happen to Babe. He had to find him. And, by what might be termed a lucky accident, he did find him.

Adjacent to the construction module they had turned into a clubhouse was a sealed hutch where Cardassian workmen had locked their tools. Not only did the Cardassians steal everything from Bajor that could be crammed into the hold of a spaceship, they were also quite proficient at pillaging from each other.

The reason Jake had bypassed the hutch was that he believed it was sealed shut. But returning to the clubhouse, Jake stumbled on a loose cable and fell against the door of the hutch, causing it to swing open.

Babe was lying on the top shelf of the hutch, keeping to the shadows. In the faint light that filtered in when Jake propped the door open, he could see Babe's golden fur. It seemed to have gotten lighter and appeared to be glowing.

Then, as he came closer, he realized that he was not seeing Babe's fur, but golden strands of silk. Jake started to touch it, then stopped. If Babe was injured, this might be part of his healing process. He didn't want to do something that would harm Babe.

Where were Nog and Dr. Bashir?

Then, as if in response to his urgent thoughts, Jake heard approaching footsteps.

"Jake?" Nog called out.

"I'm here," Jake replied, stepping out of the locker.

Nog ran up, followed by Dr. Bashir.

"You took long enough," Jake commented to Nog.

"He didn't want to come," Nog replied, glancing at Bashir. "But I said it was the only way to get you to leave the pylon."

"You have to get out of here," Dr. Bashir told Jake. "The station is under attack, and these pylons may not last much longer."

Suddenly another quake shook Deep Space Nine. This far from the center of the station, the impact was muffled, but they felt it all the same.

"What's that?" Jake asked as he regained his balance.

"Spacequakes!" Nog said. "They've been happening all over the station."

"That's why we must go now," Bashir implored.

Jake did not move. "Not without Babe." He was determined not to leave his furry friend, no matter what. He pointed inside, and Dr. Bashir entered the storage locker.

"Extraordinary."

Nog was also bewildered at what was happening to their pet. "Babe's dying!"

The Ferengi started to run to Babe, but Bashir put out an arm and gently halted him. "Wait."

Now Bashir began to act like a doctor. Holding his medical tricorder in front of him, he moved toward Babe, being careful not to alarm the creature. But there was little chance of that. Babe was occupied with other things, growing slender golden threads that were rapidly encircling his furry body.

"Do you know what's happening to him?" Jake asked, hoping the doctor could fix whatever it was that was wrong.

Bashir did not immediately reply. He was too busy analyzing the readings on his tricorder.

"This is absolutely incredible," he finally said aloud.

"What's incredible?" Nog demanded.

"Babe is—" Bashir stopped. When it came to medicine, Jake knew that the doctor was determined to be accurate in his diagnosis. Sometimes his true brilliance was concealed by his halting manner of making a statement. "I think," Bashir rephrased what he started to say, "that Babe is undergoing a transformation."

"Is that good?" Nog asked.

"A transformation?" Jake did not understand what Bashir was talking about.

"Like—" Bashir thought for a moment. "You know how a caterpillar turns into a butterfly?"

Jake and Nog stared at him. They didn't get it.

He tried again. "Babe is spinning a cocoon."

"Babe is like a caterpillar?" Jake asked.

Bashir nodded. "Yes. Exactly. Babe has reached the end of one stage of his life and is about to enter a new one."

"Like growing up?" Nog wondered.

"In a way, yes. People go from childhood to adulthood, and our bodies undergo significant changes. We call it puberty when a boy becomes a man, or a girl becomes a woman."

"But what's Babe going to become?"

"That is a very good question, Jake. But one for which I have no answer."

All during their discussion the golden threads had continued to wrap around Babe. By now he was completely enveloped in the strange cocoon. There was no sign of the furry little creature that had been their pet.

"But we'll see very soon," Bashir added.

"Doesn't it take a caterpillar a long time to become a butterfly?" Nog asked.

"Yes. But different species change at different rates. My tricorder readings indicate that Babe's metamorphosis is happening very fast." Bashir kneeled and invited the boys to do likewise. "We are about to witness one of nature's miracles."

At the same time, in another part of the space station, Commander Sisko was witnessing something quite different—the apparent destruction of Deep Space Nine.

Operations looked like a disaster zone. Broken beams were everywhere. Several wall panels had broken loose, making it difficult to move around the room. Some of the workstations were overturned. Debris littered the floor and shifted position every time another of the rumbling quakes shook the station.

Reports of similar scenes of chaos came in from the rest of Deep Space Nine. These were only terrified verbal descriptions of havoc and devastation, since many of the monitors were not working. That was what Sisko hated the most. He was nearly blind as far as the damage to his station was concerned.

"I don't understand it," O'Brien kept saying whenever he confronted a new emergency. "According to the few readout panels that are still working, nothing is wrong."

Kira scowled. "Look around, Chief. This is not nothing."

Sisko had ordered the station's phasers to return fire on the Pyxian ship. But the blasts may as well have been aimed at empty space for all the damage they did.

Dax was at a loss to explain it. "In three hundred years," the Trill officer stated, "I've never seen anything like this. It's not that the Pyxian shields are powerful. It's that their ship doesn't appear to be there at all."

At that moment another sharp quake jolted the room. The walls seemed to scream in agony from the shock.

"I don't know how much longer we're going to hold together, Commander," O'Brien said, struggling to regain his balance.

Surrounded by damaged equipment and a crew that was very close to the breaking point, Benjamin Sisko desperately needed a miracle.

A miracle was exactly what Jake and Nog were waiting for in the tool hutch in the upper docking pylon. It was what Dr. Julian Bashir had predicted. And as they watched, it began.

The cocoon that surrounded Babe was pulsating with a strange inner energy. The slender golden threads began to vibrate like the strings of a violin, making a sound unlike any they had ever heard. They covered their ears to blot out the siren wail that became so loud, it was painful. And still, the noise continued to reverberate inside their heads.

The noise was particularly painful to Nog, who could finally take it no longer and bolted from the locker.

Jake was about to follow him when he felt Bashir touch his arm. Jake responded and looked at where the doctor was pointing.

The cocoon was exploding. *No—not exploding.* Jake revised his first impression. *It was evaporating.*

The golden threads expanded and disappeared.

THE PET

Suddenly, from inside the disintegrating cocoon, a bright light shone. Jake and Bashir shielded their eyes from the light that filled the hutch like the flash from an exploding star. The light lasted less than a microsecond, yet even when he opened his eyes again, the residual effects from the flash made afterimages continue to pop in front of Jake's eyes like balloons. He thought he was blind and would never see again. But the balloons soon faded. Then, for a moment, everything was a blur. Finally his vision cleared. And what he saw was indeed a miracle.

CHAPTER 11

In Operations, Benjamin Sisko was not witnessing a miracle, but rather the violent end to a dream. This space station, constructed by Bajoran laborers for the conquering Cardassians, had become a bright beacon of hope for Bajor, a world that badly needed it. Now that dream was in danger of vanishing, along with Deep Space Nine.

And he could do nothing about it. The station was unable to either defend itself or take offensive action against this overpowering enemy.

"I just don't understand what's happening to us, Benjamin," Dax said. "None of our weapons seem to have any effect."

"It's like playing a hologame," O'Brien added. "Except this is for real."

"For real—" Sisko started to say something, then stopped as another shock wave rolled through Operations.

Regaining his balance, Sisko looked over at the frightened figure of Darm, sitting where Odo had left him, held captive by pressure loops that encircled his ankles. The commander agreed with Odo that the *Ulysses* spacer appeared to be partly responsible for their plight. It had been confirmed that Darm had indeed landed an unauthorized runabout on one of the Pyxian moons.

But under questioning, Darm denied any knowledge of the Pyxian prince. He would perish along with everyone else on the station if he refused to tell the truth. Yet he remained stoic in his denial.

Meanwhile, reports of mass destruction continued to come in from all parts of the station. The fact that no one had been injured, except for some self-inflicted wounds when the crowds panicked, was remarkable. It was also very strange.

"This whole situation is very strange," Sisko said aloud to no one in particular. "It's almost as if—"

"Dad!"

Sisko turned and was startled to see his son standing in the open doorway of the turbolift.

"Jake," Sisko said. "You don't belong here."

"It's all right, Commander." Julian Bashir emerged to join Jake. They were followed by Nog.

It was then that Sisko noticed someone else in the turbolift, someone the commander did not recognize.

Bashir looked over his shoulder at the stranger. "Sir, may I present His Highness, the Pyxian royal prince."

Sisko saw a youth, about Jake's age, tall and slender as a Zylian wind reed. He was humanoid in appearance,

but covered from head to foot with purple pebbled skin.

"I am"—the boy paused, glanced over at Jake and Nog, then smiled as he turned again to face Sisko. "I am the one you called Babe."

"I don't understand," O'Brien said.

"I think Dr. Bashir can explain," Sisko said.

Bashir smiled the way he did whenever he had the opportunity to display his intelligence. "The being we knew as Babe was—like a caterpillar that has now changed into a butterfly."

"That's incredible." O'Brien tried to grasp the concept.

Sisko rubbed his chin. "I can't call you Babe anymore. What do I call you?"

"My true name is Joryl," the boy that had been Babe replied. He looked over at the spacer Darm, who was shackled in the corner. "That one took me from my home before the Solitary—my time of changing—was complete."

At that moment another quake shook the room.

Sisko stumbled, then quickly regained his balance. "I suggest we dispense with further explanations for the time being." He looked at Joryl. "Can you help us stop this destruction before Deep Space Nine is totally demolished?"

Joryl nodded. He stepped to the communication terminal. "This is Joryl of the Line."

"You are safe, my prince?" the reply echoed in the room.

"I am safe, Admiral. Let what has been done be undone."

"By your command, it will be so."

A blinding flash of light filled Operations. The intense glare lasted for an instant, and when it was gone everything in the station was exactly as it had been before the attack began.

"Ops was a shambles. Now it's normal!" Kira observed the transformation with amazement.

Jake could see on the now-functioning display screens that everything on the space station—from the Promenade to the most remote docking bays—was also back to normal, as if nothing had ever happened.

"How is this possible?" O'Brien asked.

"Because," Joryl said, "it never did happen. All that you saw—you saw in your minds. It was not real." Joryl explained to Commander Sisko, "We Pyxians are a peaceful race."

"Peaceful," Kira grumbled. "You almost destroyed our station."

"Not really, Major," Sisko said. "It was all an illusion."

"That's a trick I'd like to learn," Nog said.

"Then we were never in any real danger?" Kira asked.

Joryl hesitated. "Not exactly. Although the Pyxians, using our mind-boosters, are only projecting an artificial reality—like in your own holosuites—the experience is still real to those involved in the illusion."

"In other words, if your people had 'destroyed' Deep

Space Nine, the trauma of that experience would have been devastating to everyone on board," Bashir said.

Joryl nodded. "I am afraid that is correct."

"Why," Sisko wondered, "did your admiral not just beam aboard so we could discuss the matter—before it led to hostilities, even if the attack wasn't real?"

"Ours is a very private race, Commander. Our only real defense is our ability to camouflage ourselves. Direct contact of any kind makes us vulnerable. We avoid it at all costs." Joryl rose. "But I must leave now. My Solitary period is ended, and my people await their prince."

Jake went over to this alien youth who now stood slightly taller than himself. "It's kind of weird looking up at you instead of down."

Joryl smiled at Jake. "Jake, I will not forget you. Or you, Nog." He included Nog in his smile. "Nor the friendship that both of you offered to me."

"We won't forget you, either," Jake replied. "You may not be our pet any longer, but you'll always be our friend."

Watching his father accompany Joryl to the Ops transporter, Jake felt as if something big and important was walking out of his life, and he felt lonely. He looked over and saw from Nog's expression that his Ferengi friend obviously felt as bad about Joryl's leaving Deep Space Nine as he did.

"Perhaps we will see you again, Joryl," Sisko said as Joryl reached the transporter platform.

"Perhaps you will, Commander. This may be the moment for the Pyxians to begin reaching out to other life forms."

"You're welcome here any time," Jake said as he felt in his pocket. After a moment of hesitation he took a well-worn baseball from it and tossed it to Joryl.

The prince plucked the object from the air and looked at it with pleasure. He, Jake, and Nog smiled at one another.

"Thank you," Joryl said. "I will always treasure this token from the two who befriended a stranger in their midst."

Joryl entered the transporter, then turned to O'Brien, who was at the control panel. "I am ready."

"One to beam out," O'Brien said and touched the control panel.

The electronic beam enveloped the Pyxian royal prince, turning his lizard-like body to atoms. He vanished.

"Goodbye, Babe," Jake said quietly.

CHAPTER 12

The fans at Yankee Stadium roared. It was three balls and two strikes. Bottom of the ninth. The visitors were hanging on to a precarious one-run lead.

Babe Ruth signaled for time and stepped away from the plate. He swung his bat in a vicious arc that cut through the oppressive July heat like a knife.

He stepped back to the plate. He was ready.

The Babe looked toward the pitcher's mound wearing a confident smile.

Outwardly young Jake Sisko appeared equally confident. But inside his stomach was doing cartwheels. This was it. The game was all riding on him and his next pitch.

Play it smart, Jake told himself. *He's anticipating your fastball, so give him something else, something simple.*

Jake glanced over at his father in the dugout, then at the new batboy—Nog. Now he wound up and stepped forward as he released the ball.

He threw a slow curveball that was aimed at the inside corner. It was the pitch he had been practicing in the cornfield with Nog and Babe—the other Babe. It was his smartest pitch. But not smart enough.

This Babe in the Yankee uniform must have been waiting for just this pitch. The crack of the bat against the ball echoed through the stadium like a bomb exploding.

The ball whistled past Jake's ear, gaining altitude as it roared toward deep center field. There seemed to be no way to stop it from clearing the fence. But then, as the ball appeared to be going, going, gone—someone leaped high into the air and came down with it.

Babe. The little rhinolike creature caught the sure home run in his mouth. Then, as he floated back to earth, he transformed into the humanoid figure of the prince.

"You're out!" the prince yelled as he landed on the outfield grass.

Jake turned to his father with a broad smile. "Thanks, Dad. It's a nice surprise to see Babe in the holosuite."

The elder Sisko removed his manager's cap and scratched his head. "I'm as surprised as you are, son." He looked over at Nog. "Did you play with the program, Nog?"

"No, Commander Sisko. I didn't. I swear it wasn't me."

The prince smiled as he strolled to the pitcher's mound. "I'm not one of your holosuite illusions," he said as he tossed the baseball to Jake.

"It's really you? But I thought you were on your way back to Pyx?"

"Actually I am. But we Pyxians can project replicas of ourselves across many light-years, even through a wormhole. Thought has no dimension."

The prince looked around at the cheering crowd that filled Yankee Stadium. Even if the home team had lost, they loved their baseball.

"This is a game I do not quite understand," the prince told Jake, "but it is one that I enjoy—in both my forms."

"I wish you could stay here," Jake said, but he already knew that wasn't possible.

"I must go. But I leave you a token to remember me by."

And with that he winked out of existence.

Commander Sisko and Nog approached the pitcher's mound. Nog was pointing at something. Jake saw that he was pointing at the baseball in his hand.

Only it was not a baseball.

It was the size and shape of a baseball. But rather than white, rainbows ran over its surface as they had on the gigantic ship and on Oryx's helmet. An inner light gave the sphere a life of its own. Jake stared down at the softly glowing orb. As he turned it, inside he could see faint images, first of the furry little rhino and then of the tall young prince. Jake seemed to hear a voice that echoed in his mind: *I will be with you always, my friends.*

He looked over and saw from Nog's smile that he, too, heard the voice.

Commander Sisko put one arm around Jake's shoulder and the other around Nog's. "Let's go home, boys. I'm treating each of you to a Ventaxan Volcano Sundae."

They walked toward where they knew the holosuite door was located. "Computer, freeze program," Sisko said.

"And save," Jake added.

About the Authors

MEL GILDEN has written two novels set in the Star Trek universe—*Boogeymen,* a Star Trek: The Next Generation novel, and *The Starship Trap,* which features the original crew of the *U.S.S. Enterprise.* Many of his books, such as *Surfing Samurai Robots,* take place outside of the Star Trek universe. He's also written many books for kids, including the *Fifth Grade Monsters* series, the *My Brother Blubb* series (available from Minstrel Books), and his latest hardcover, *The Pumpkins of Time.* He's also written animated cartoons and hosted radio shows. Mel is hard at work on his next Deep Space Nine adventure for young readers. What a guy!

TED PEDERSEN used to be a computer programmer in Seattle, but made the long trek south to Los Angeles, where he has been writing science fiction for the past dozen years in the wacky world of animated cartoons. Most recently he has written TV episodes for *X-Men, Cadillacs & Dinosaurs, ExoSquad,* and the upcoming *Marvel Comics Action Hour.* He is also working on his own Deep Space Nine adventure for young readers. He lives in Venice, California, with one wife, two computers, and several cats.

About the Illustrator

TODD CAMERON HAMILTON is a self-taught artist who has resided all his life in Chicago, Illinois. He has been a professional illustrator for the past ten years, specializing in fantasy, science fiction, and horror. Todd is the current president of the Association of Science Fiction and Fantasy Artists. His original works grace many private and corporate collections. He has co-authored two novels and several short stories. When not drawing, painting, or writing, his interests include metalsmithing, puppetry, and teaching.

STAR TREK®
—GENERATIONS™—

A Novel by John Vornholt
Based on STAR TREK GENERATIONS
Story by Rick Berman & Ronald D. Moore & Brannon Braga
Screenplay by Ronald D. Moore & Brannon Braga

Available from

POCKET
BOOKS

A MINSTREL® BOOK